The Rewrite Circle

The Rewrite Circle

Archana R Singh

THE BROWSER

Title: The Rewrite Circle
Author: Archana R Singh

ISBN: 978-93-47590-05-4

Published by:
JGS Enterprises Pvt Ltd
Imprint: The Browser

Publisher's Address:
SCO 14-15, FF, Sector 8-C, Chandigarh 160 009

Website: thebrowser.org
Email: service@thebrowser.org

© Layout and Cover Design by beagles
99beagles.com

Contents

Contents

Reclaiming Life

Five women. Five stories. One unexpected friendship.

They came to America to be near their NRI children, anchored by duty, caught between continents, and quietly fading into the background. But when they meet in Seattle, something shifts.

An impulsive journey to Alaska confronts them with aspects of themselves long hidden. Through confessions and cups of chai, these women create a circle of trust—and start to rewrite the rules of who they are permitted to be.

The Rewrite Circle is a tender, witty novel about second chances, unexpected friendships, and the quiet power of women reclaiming life on their own terms.

CHAPTER 1

Footprints on the Sands of Time

Sugandha

Cradled gently by the Bay of Bengal lies Machilipatnam, a coastal town in Andhra Pradesh.

It was put on the map by the Vijayawada-Machilipatnam railway line, since 1908—a piece of information that grandfathers wielded like a trophy while the younger generation barely batted an eyelid. The railway station resembled a colonial-era storybook—whitewashed, with red trims, and inhabited by pigeons who thought they paid the rent.

Flanking the tracks was a row of squat railway quarters, homes that had seen decades and never had a makeover. Each had a tiny kitchen garden, a patch of rebellious spinach, and the sweet scent of Mallepuvvu—jasmine—travelled with the breeze.

In one of these corners lived the Reddy family. They had the honour of growing the most fragrant jasmine shrubs in the railway quarters. Women came from nearby homes to pluck a few flowers for their braids, making the Reddy compound the 'go-to' place in Machilipatnam. Mr Venkata Samy Reddy, a railway clerk, was dependable and humble. He walked across the bridge to the railway station every morning with his daughter, Sugandha, trailing behind him.

Sugandha was the kind of child who made every school photograph look lovely. Her mother wanted to give her a fancy name, not the usual local nickname. So instead of Mallelu, which was her grandmother's choice, they chose Sugandha. It sounded classy, cosmopolitan, and just fragrant enough. Her school was conveniently located right across the railway tracks. Every day, she trotted along in a navy-blue uniform, her braids swaying, her water bottle bouncing, and a Mallepuvvu tucked firmly into her hair.

Life in Machilipatnam was about balance—old-school traditions and newfangled modernity constantly jostled for space. The Reddy household was structured in routine. Mornings were for aartis, evenings for plucking flowers, and nights for studying under tube lights that buzzed like confused bees.

And then came the ninth standard, when life stopped following the schedule.

It began innocently enough. Sanjay was the new boy in school—a Punjabi boy with a mop of brown hair that looked like the wind had styled it as he rode his red, fashionable cycle. His father was the new station master, which made Sanjay railway royalty.

He was complete hero material—singing songs, giving roses to the girls, and the works. Sugandha found herself smiling when he hummed songs to her.

One day, her friend, Rupa, burst in, dramatic as always. 'Sugandha! *Ek Duje Ke Liye* is playing at the theatre tonight! We HAVE to go!'

Sugandha, mid-homework, looked up excitedly, 'Really? Kamal Hassan?'

Rupa nodded, already plotting. 'I talked to your parents. Don't worry. Aunty even packed us *murukkus* for the road.'

At the theatre, Sugandha spotted Sanjay and his family on the balcony. Their eyes met for a moment—the point where hundreds of violins play in the background with a *la la la la la la la la....* Rupa noticed, of course.

'Was that Sanjay? And did he just telepathically sing a song to you?'

'No! Maybe. Stop it!'

But Sanjay didn't stop. The next morning, he was back at it. Leaning against a wall, singing, '*Tere mere beech mein...*' like the hallway was his stage and Sugandha was the only one in the audience.

Rupa elbowed her. 'You, my friend, are in a love story!'

Sugandha tried to deny it, but her cheeks had turned beetroot.

Soon, Sanjay's friends were cornering her with earnest speeches: 'He's smart, he's kind, and have you seen him at rifle shooting? He's the Amitabh of our batch.'

Sugandha tried to maintain composure, but Sanjay's sideways glances and soft humming turned her knees into jelly.

After the school fete, where he won her teddy bears and paid for the merry-go-round, she was done for. She began waiting for him, timing her walks to catch him cycling by, and even inventing reasons to walk slower. She began to avoid crossing the bridge with her father.

As per his schedule, every morning, Mr Reddy, with a crisp white shirt neatly tucked, took his customary walk over the bridge to the railway station. That morning, his old colleague, Nageshwar Rao, stepped beside him, clearing his throat in a way that suggested he had news.

'Reddy *Garu*,' Rao began, adjusting his spectacles, 'I need to talk to you about Sugandha.'

Mr Reddy's steps faltered—just a fraction—but he recovered quickly. 'What is it, Rao? Everything alright?'

Rao exhaled as if bracing himself. 'It's about a boy. Sanjay. He's been… very attentive towards Sugandha.'

'Attentive?' Mr Reddy's eyebrows did a slow, suspicious arch. 'What kind of attention?'

Rao winced. 'Singing songs, sneaking roses into her books…. It's become quite the topic among the students.'

Mr Reddy inhaled sharply. 'And Sugandha? What's she doing in all this?'

Rao gave him a small, knowing smile. 'Well… she's shy, but she's not exactly telling him to get lost.'

Mr Reddy exhaled through his nose, his jaw tightening.

Rao patted his shoulder in a fatherly, been-there, done-that way. 'Teenagers, Reddy *Garu.* They'll do these things. She's a good girl. This will pass.'

As they reached the station, Mr Reddy's face was calm, but his mind was racing. That evening, the carefully maintained decorum of the Reddy household teetered on the edge of collapse.

The living room, usually a haven for evening coffee and quiet conversation, was thick with tension—even the aroma of freshly brewed filter *kaapi* couldn't cut through it.

'Sugandha,' Mr Reddy began, his voice clipped, 'your mother and I need to talk to you.'

Sugandha, who had been blissfully dunking a Marie biscuit into her coffee, suddenly sat up, her senses tingling. Uh-oh. That tone never meant good news.

'Yes, *Nanna*?'

Her mother reached out, giving her arm a small, reassuring pat. 'Mr Rao mentioned something today,' she said, her voice all honey and diplomacy. 'About a boy. Sanjay.'

Sanjay. Oh God.

Sugandha's fingers tightened around the edge of her dupatta as heat crept up her neck. 'Uh… yes, he… um… he has been trying to get my attention.'

Mr Reddy exploded.

'Trying to get your attention? He's been belting out songs and showering you with roses! What is this—some *filmi tamasha*?'

Sugandha shrank into her seat. 'I—I didn't encourage him! I didn't know what to do!'

'Didn't know what to do? You should have told us immediately! Do you realise what people will say? What about our family's reputation?'

Her mother tried the soothing wife approach. '*Emandi*, please, let's talk calmly—'

But Mr Reddy was on a roll. 'No, this is unacceptable! You are too young for this nonsense! Studies, the future, is what you should think about—not some Romeo!'

Sugandha's eyes filled with tears. 'I'm sorry, *Nanna*. I never meant for this to happen.'

Mr Reddy took a deep breath, his anger still simmering but slightly reined in. 'You must understand the seriousness of this. We trust you. But you tell him next time—no more roses or songs. This stops now.'

Sugandha nodded quickly, her heart still hammering. 'Yes, *Nanna*. I'll focus on my studies. I promise.'

Her mother gave her hand a comforting squeeze. 'That's our good girl. Just be careful, okay?'

Mr Reddy exhaled, the fire in his eyes dimming slightly. 'Fine. Let's eat. The matter is closed.'

The matter was far from being over. It had only just begun.

Sugandha and Sanjay had mastered the fine art of deception for two glorious years.

Every evening, she'd toss out a casual '*Amma*, I am going to study at Rupa's house', and off she'd go—straight past the market, past the chatty flower vendors, and towards their banyan tree, where Sanjay would be waiting. Under the tangled roots and rustling leaves, their conversations were a giddy mix of flirtation, awkward silences, and deep, dreamy sighs.

Some days, they wandered through the town's narrow lanes, stealing moments in dimly lit tea stalls where the spiced chai was as intoxicating as their whispered promises. At other times, it was just a smile across a crowded classroom, a note slipped into a textbook, or a stolen touch as they passed each other in the corridors.

One sweltering April evening, just as Sugandha was pretending to study while secretly rereading Sanjay's latest love note, doom struck.

From the living room, her father could be heard speaking to her mother.

'Rama, did you hear? Mr Chopra has been transferred back to Hyderabad. His assignment is done. He's leaving next week.'

Sugandha froze. Hyderabad? Next week?!

Her mother sounded only mildly interested. 'Really? That's sudden.'

Her father sighed. 'Yes, but the new track is ready. And they need him there for another project.'

Rama, ever practical, said, 'We should invite them for dinner before they leave.'

Sugandha, clutching Sanjay's note in her now sweaty palm, knew one thing—she had to see him. NOW.

Sanjay was waiting for her outside the school gate the following day, leaning against his cycle. As soon as he saw her, his face broke into a perfect smile.

She hurried over, her breath coming fast. 'Sanjay—why didn't you tell me?'

Sanjay's jaw tightened. 'I know. I found out yesterday. It's happening too fast, Sugandha. I don't know what to do.'

She nodded, her voice wobbly. 'My parents are inviting your family for dinner before you go.'

Sanjay's eyes widened. 'Oh God! Our dads have been working on the project together.'

Sugandha chewed her lip. 'What happens to us?'

Sanjay took her hand, his grip warm and firm. 'We figure it out. Remember Vasu and Sapna in *Ek Duje Ke Liye*? They lived apart but never stopped loving each other.'

She gave him a pointed look. 'Yes, and they JUMPED OFF A CLIFF, Sanjay!'

Sanjay grinned. 'Okay, except for that part. We'll write a new ending.'

And as they walked to class, fingers entwined, their hearts swayed between love and uncertainty—one last week of stolen moments before reality came knocking.

The dinner was set with care, the aroma of rich, home-cooked dishes filling the air. Sugandha's family welcomed the Chopras warmly, unaware of the storm brewing beneath the surface. Mr Reddy, with a polite smile, led Mr Chopra and his family to the table.

The dinner started pleasantly. The men were discussing railway tracks, while the women exchanged recipes, and Sugandha pretended not to notice Sanjay sitting dangerously close to her.

And then, it all went downhill.

Mr Reddy turned to Sanjay, his tone genial. 'So, young man, which class are you in?'

Sanjay, gripping his spoon like a lifeline, cleared his throat. 'Twelfth standard, sir.'

'And what's your name?'

Before Sanjay could answer, Mr Chopra jumped in with a rare display of parental awareness. 'His name is Sanjay, Reddy *Garu*. My son.'

A complete pin-drop silence followed. Sugandha had never seen her father go from *idli*-soft to gunpowder chutney so fast. His expression hardened.

'Sanjay… your son?'

Ever the domestic diplomat, Rama looked back and forth between the two men, her brow furrowed. '*Emandi*, what's the matter?'

Mr Reddy exhaled sharply, then turned to Mr Chopra with all the menace of a high-speed locomotive. 'I've heard things. About your son. And my daughter. And how they've been… fraternising.'

Mr Chopra's face went red. 'What are you implying, Reddy *Garu*? They're kids! Whatever they shared, it was innocent.'

'Innocent? Innocent?!' Mr Reddy thundered. 'Love notes, roses, school-corridor serenades? This is NOT how we raised our daughter!'

Sanjay, deciding it was time to salvage the situation, leaned forward. 'Sir, I never meant to cause any trouble. I truly care—'

But Mr Reddy was too far gone. 'Care? You're just a boy! You have no idea what you're talking about!'

Mrs Chopra, sensing that things were one plate throw away from a full-blown disaster, pushed back her chair. 'I think we should leave.'

Mr Chopra nodded, his mouth set in a grim line. 'Come, Sanjay.'

Sanjay's heart plummeted as he looked at Sugandha. She was already blinking back tears.

'Sugandha, I—'

But before she could respond, Mr Reddy's voice sliced through the room like a cleaver. 'No. More. Words. This ends here.'

The Chopras exited in a huff, the door slamming behind them like a final nail in the coffin of young love.

And Sugandha? She just stood there, the weight of the evening pressing down on her, knowing that her love story had just come to an unceremonious, heartbreaking halt.

The house was too quiet.

Sugandha felt it pressing down on her as she entered the yard.

The night was thick with humidity and heartbreak. A train was pulling out of the station—slow at first, reluctant, like it knew it was leaving something behind. The whistle cut through the dark, long and final. The guard swung his lantern. Up. Down. Up. Down. The light flickered like a goodbye.

Sugandha swallowed hard and went back inside.

She yanked out her tape recorder, shoved in a cassette, and pressed play.

'*Tere mere beech mein, kaisa hai yeh bandhan, anjaana....*'

Lata Mangeshkar's voice filled the room, tugging at all the wrong places in her heart. She pressed rewind. Played it again.

'*Tere mere beech mein, kaisa hai yeh bandhan, anjaana....*'

Rewind. Play.

Somewhere between the fourth and fifth replay, the tape betrayed her. It hiccupped, twisted, and then, just like her love story, became entirely entangled.

And that was it. That was her final straw.

She let out a choked sob, curled into herself, and cried her heart out.

Machilipatnam moved on. The trains came and went. Jasmine bloomed. Mr Reddy resumed his morning walks.

But somewhere, in an old school notebook, a dried Mallepuvvu lay hidden between love notes and unsent letters. A little fragrant proof that once upon a time, love had blossomed by the tracks.

Debjyoti

'Debu, Debu!' Shanta called out again, her voice both insistent and tinged with irritation.

She stood at the threshold of their bungalow, wiping her hands on her apron, watching her daughter stubbornly perched on the garden swing. The late afternoon sun cast a golden glow on the lush green lawn, but all Shanta could think about was the clock ticking inside the house. There was so much to do before the evening party—guests to welcome, food to prepare, and Debu, as usual, was in no hurry to cooperate.

'Rani, how long has she been on that swing?' Shanta called out.

'Since after lunch, *Boudi*,' Rani replied, her arms aching but still patient as she pushed Debu, who squealed in delight.

'Debu! Come down now,' Shanta said firmly. 'We need to get you ready for the party, and Rani didi has work inside.'

Three-year-old Debu clutched the ropes tighter. 'No, Ma! Just one more swing!'

'One more? That's what you said ten swings ago!' Shanta sighed.

Rani Didi shrugged. '*Uni shunben na, Boudi*. (She won't listen, Madam.)'

Shanta folded her arms. 'If you don't come down, no *laddus* at the party!'

Debu's eyes widened. 'No *laddus*?' she gasped.

'No *laddus*,' Shanta confirmed.

Torn between the swing and sweets, Debu finally let go. 'Okay, Ma... but just for the *laddus*,' she muttered.

Shanta scooped her up with a smile. 'Good girl! Now, let's get you ready.'

As they walked inside, Debu peeked back. 'Tomorrow, Ma? Can I swing tomorrow?'

Shanta chuckled. 'Yes, but tomorrow we're going to Kolkata to meet *Dadu* and *Dida*. And tonight, my baby, you're the star of the evening!'

Debu giggled, forgetting her rebellion as Shanta carried her inside.

The Barrackpore Cantonment, with its majestic Gulmohars, wide roads, and stoic colonial bungalows, stood like an island outside Kolkata's chaos. Though the city was a train ride away, life here moved slowly, measuredly, and brass plates and flower beds flourished.

Families like the Bannerjis lived in neat, close-knit units. Children cycled on empty streets, played in sprawling gardens, and returned to homes where the order of cantonment life met the warmth of family chaos.

Major Bannerji's bungalow, with its chipped white paint and wraparound veranda, was one such home. His wife, Shanta, ran it with military discipline yet effortless warmth, tending to her roses and hibiscus with the same care as her household. But the real treasure was the creaky porch swing, where their daughter, little Debu, spent hours shrieking joyfully as Rani pushed her higher.

Major Bannerji was the quintessential army man—calm, disciplined, and unflappable. Always poised and prepared for the next posting, Shanta transformed every house into a home.

And then there was Debu, a firecracker of a child with mischievous eyes and boundless energy. Whether chasing butterflies, playing hide-and-seek, or swinging with wild abandon, she lit up the house with her giggles, her laughter echoing through the veranda—the true heart of the Bannerji home.

Life in the cantonment felt safe, secure, and almost like a storybook, as if nothing could ever go wrong there. It was a small family in a perfect world—or so they believed.

That sunny morning was no different. The family was all set for their trip to Kolkata to visit Major Bannerji's ageing parents. Bags were packed, Shanta had double-checked everything, and Debu, excited to see her grandparents, ran around clutching her favourite toy. They left their tranquil cantonment home and headed to Barrackpore railway station.

The platform bustled with activity—hawkers selling snacks, porters hauling luggage, and families saying hurried goodbyes. Debu, still full of excitement, clung to her mother's hand, her eyes wide with curiosity.

'Debu, hold my hand, don't run off,' Shanta said, adjusting her sari as she balanced their bags in one hand, her eyes scanning the crowded platform.

'Look, Ma! Train!' Debu squealed excitedly, tugging at Shanta's hand. Her wide eyes sparkled joyfully.

Major Bannerji chuckled, patting her head. 'Yes, we're going to see *Dadu* and *Dida*, remember?'

As they prepared to board the train, Debu suddenly fell on the platform, her body crumpling like a rag doll onto the cold stone. Shanta's scream sliced through the air, piercing the normalcy of their day. She dropped everything, her hands trembling as she knelt beside her child. Major Bannerji stood frozen, disbelief hitting him like a wave, before instinct kicked in. He scooped up Debu's limp form, his heart hammering wildly in his chest, while Shanta staggered after him, her voice a broken whisper, 'Debu, Debu, please....'

They sped through the tree-lined roads, Shanta clutching their daughter's tiny, lifeless hand, muttering frantic prayers between sobs. Major Bannerji's grip on the wheel tightened with each second, the familiar scenery now warped by terror. The calm streets and manicured lawns now felt cruel, mocking the nightmare unfolding.

The small military hospital swallowed them in its cold, sterile embrace. The ticking of the clock echoed in the hallway as the doctor's grave face blurred before their eyes. Minutes stretched into unbearable hours, the weight of fear pressing down on them. Shanta clung to Major Bannerji, their silence louder than any words they could muster.

When the doctor finally spoke, the words landed like a punch.

'Your daughter has had a heart attack.'

Shanta's knees buckled, her breath leaving her as Major Bannerji caught her, his mind reeling. A heart attack? At three years old? It was incomprehensible, a cruelty they couldn't fathom. Debu lay in the hospital bed, tubes and machines surrounding her tiny body, her laughter replaced by the mechanical beeping that now measured her life.

Back home, the silence was deafening. The swing on the porch sat still, abandoned. The once-bright flowers in the garden now seemed to droop in mourning. The house felt hollow, stripped of the warmth Debu's giggles had filled it with. Shanta wandered through it like a ghost, the days bleeding into nights, each visit to the hospital another stab of fear.

After a week in the hospital, the Bannerjis, with the support of their friends and family, were coming to grips with the news of Debu's illness. On the day of her release from the hospital, assuming that the worst was over, they prepared to take Debu home.

With a furrowed brow and a kind yet firm demeanour, Colonel Rai, the army doctor, approached them after a thorough examination.

Major Bannerji leapt forward to shake his hand, 'Thank you, Sir!'

The doctor cleared his throat and began, his voice steady but sombre. 'Mrs and Major Bannerji, we've conducted preliminary tests, and it's clear that Debu is suffering from a serious heart condition.'

Shanta's heart sank. 'What's wrong with her? Is she going to be okay?'

The doctor's gaze was compassionate but unwavering. 'Debu has a condition known as an atrial septal defect—a hole in the wall between the two upper chambers of her heart. This defect is causing significant strain on her heart and needs urgent attention.'

Major Bannerji's face grew pale. 'What does she need?'

The doctor continued, 'To correct this defect, she will need open-heart surgery. We don't have the specialised facilities here to perform such a procedure. I recommend transferring her to a multi-speciality hospital with the expertise and equipment for this surgery. Such facilities are available in either PGIMER (Post Graduate Institute of Medical Education and Research), Chandigarh or CMC (Christian Medical College), Vellore.'

Shanta gasped, clutching her chest. 'A surgery? But she's so young—'

'I understand this is overwhelming,' the doctor said gently. 'But time is of the essence. The sooner we get her to the right facility, the better her chances of recovery.'

Major Bannerji nodded, his mind racing. 'We'll do whatever it takes.'

The doctor's expression softened. 'I'll ensure everything is arranged once we know where you can transfer yourself. I suggest you begin the transfer procedure, which takes time.'

Shanta broke into tears, her body shaking with the weight of her fears. Major Bannerji stood beside her, trying to offer comfort, but his heart was heavy with dread. Their little girl's life now hung in the balance, and they could only hope for a miracle as they prepared for the long, uncertain journey ahead.

The following day, Major Bannerji, clutching a sheaf of papers tightly, made determined strides towards the commanding officer, Brigadier Kataria's office. The office door was slightly ajar as he approached, and he could hear the murmur of conversation inside. He took a deep breath, squared his shoulders, and knocked firmly before entering.

Brigadier Kataria looked up from his desk, his face lined with the experience of many years of service. He gestured for Major

Bannerji to come in. 'Major Bannerji, what brings you here at this hour?'

Major Bannerji stepped in and saluted his senior officer, his face a mix of urgency and resolve. 'Sir, I need to discuss something critical regarding my daughter's health.'

Brigadier Kataria motioned him to sit. 'Of course. What's the situation?'

Major Bannerji sat down and placed the documents on the desk. 'Sir, my daughter, Debu, has been diagnosed with a serious heart condition—a hole in the heart. The doctors here recommend that she undergo open-heart surgery at a specialised facility.'

The brigadier's expression shifted to one of concern. 'And where do you need her transferred?'

'As per the doctor's advice,' Major Bannerji said, 'the two most suitable hospitals are Chandigarh and Vellore. The PGI in Chandigarh has the necessary facilities and expertise to handle her case. I request a compassionate transfer to Chandigarh so Debu can receive her specialised care.'

Brigadier Kataria glanced at the papers, which detailed Debu's medical condition and the recommendation for specialised treatment. He nodded thoughtfully, his gaze returning to Major Bannerji.

"I understand how urgent this is. Immediate action is required. However, transferring to a location like Chandigarh involves logistical and administrative considerations.'

Major Bannerji's voice was steady but laced with desperation. 'Sir, I'm fully prepared to handle the logistics and make any necessary arrangements. I need your approval to facilitate this transfer on compassionate grounds.'

Brigadier Kataria leaned back in his chair, weighing the request carefully. 'Major Bannerji, I'll be honest, this isn't a standard procedure. However, given the gravity of your daughter's condition and the situation's urgency, I'm prepared to support this transfer.'

The brigadier picked up the phone and called the appropriate channels. After a brief conversation, he hung up and turned to Major Bannerji with a reassuring nod.

'The transfer to Chandigarh is approved in principle. Paperwork will follow. I've instructed the relevant departments to expedite the process and provide you with all necessary support. I hope for the best for your daughter.'

Major Bannerji's face lit up with a mixture of relief and gratitude. 'Thank you, Sir. Your support means the world to us.'

Brigadier Kataria's expression softened. 'Take care of your family, Bannerji. We'll ensure that everything is handled swiftly.'

As Major Bannerji left the office, clutching the approved papers, a wave of hope mingled with his anxiety. The road ahead remained uncertain, but Brigadier Kataria's support and the imminent transfer to Chandigarh offered a glimmer of optimism in their darkest hour.

The rest of the days passed in a haze. They were busy packing and planning for the long trip to Chandigarh. According to their army entitlement, they would have to take the train. Since there was no direct train, they would need to travel to Kolkata, then onward to New Delhi, and finally to Chandigarh. It was a long journey ahead, which took three days to complete.

Finally, the day of departure arrived. The sky was painted in twilight orange hues as the sun's last rays gently kissed the rooftops of the small military quarters. The family's car was packed with a jumble of bags, medical documents, and the emotional weight of a heart-wrenching journey. Major Bannerji and Shanta conducted a last-minute check of their belongings, their faces etched with worry and resolve.

Rani, the family's loyal housekeeper, stood by the car, her usually composed demeanour cracking under strain. Her eyes were red-rimmed, and her hands trembled as she clutched a small, worn-out cloth—a token of her affection for Debu. As Shanta approached her, Rani's carefully held composure crumbled. Tears welled up in her eyes, and she hugged little Debu.

'*Boudi*, I can't bear to see you leave like this,' she choked out, her voice breaking. 'I've watched Debu grow up from a tiny baby to this brave little girl, and now she's facing something frightening.'

Equally emotional, Shanta touched Rani's shoulder, her tears mingling with Rani's. 'Rani, we're doing everything we can to help Debu. Your prayers and love mean a great deal to us. We need to stay hopeful and strong.'

Debu, now sitting in the back seat with a soft blanket draped over her, watched the exchange with a quiet, understanding gaze.

She reached out a small hand, her voice silky yet firm. 'Rani *Didi*, don't cry. I'll be okay. I promise.'

Rani's tears flowed freely as she knelt by the car, taking Debu's hand. 'You're a brave little girl, Debu. I'll be praying for you every single day. May God protect you.'

As the car doors closed and the engine started, Rani stood by, her face a picture of concern and hope. The car pulled away, leaving a cloud of dust and an emotional farewell.

In the fading light, Rani watched until the car was a mere speck on the horizon.

Sonali

The first time Chandra saw her baby girl, she was filled with only one thought: 'She is mine.' It was a Mangalorean-type morning in Kudroli, meaning everything smelled vaguely of coconut, incense, and something burning on the stove. Chandra lay on a creaky wooden cot, surrounded by flustered aunties, a nurse who looked like she'd rather be anywhere else, and her sister-in-law, Pushpa, who had taken it upon herself to manage the situation.

'We must have a naming ceremony *immediately*! *Muhurat* is very good today. Planetary alignments like this don't come often,' Pushpa said, looking suspiciously like she had insider tips from Saturn.

Chandra, still exhausted, offered a weak smile.

Across town, in a quieter, cooler corner of Kudroli, Clara was lighting a candle at St. Anthony's Church. Clara was Chandra's best friend and was the kind of woman who never raised her voice but always got the last word. She whispered a prayer: 'Let this baby be clever. Or at least charming. Either one is enough in this world!'

That's how her life began, wrapped in a blanket, smudged with sandalwood paste, kissed by every woman in the family and their friends.

The naming ceremony itself was an overfed affair. There were too many flowers, too many *laddus*, and too much noise. Pushpa had pre-rehearsed her lines and announced them dramatically.

'We name this little bundle of sunshine... *Sonali*. Golden girl, our family's very own sunrise.'

Sonali sneezed.

The pooja concluded in a blur of turmeric and abundant parenting advice. Chandra received a copper tumbler of *jeera* water and was told that she must eat twelve almonds daily if she wanted Sonali to excel in Math. Clara arrived soon after with a box of homemade rose cookies and a gentle kiss for the baby's forehead.

'She'll be a handful,' Clara said, 'just like you.'

As Sonali grew up, she had one foot in the temple and one in the church. Her mother sang bhajans while Clara taught her how to say grace before meals. She knew how to make *modak* with her grandmother and microwave popcorn with perfect timing. Her accent shifted from a Konkani sing-song to crisp English, depending on who was listening. She prayed to God for good marks but occasionally blamed Him for her bad hair days.

People always said she was a lucky child—born on an auspicious day, named with ceremony, and raised with equal parts logic and love. But Sonali knew that she had been born to a woman who took no nonsense, loved deeply, and believed that if all else failed, a hot cup of filter coffee and a fresh bedsheet could solve almost everything. She thought it so fiercely that she internalised it. She also knew that what her mother would miss, Clara Aunty could clarify for her! She had once mentioned it to her, 'Clara is for clarification!' Clara Aunty had smiled benevolently.

Sonali had always been a curious child, the kind who couldn't accept a 'because I said so' without protesting. During bedtime stories, she sat up, frowning, wondering how a pumpkin could support the weight of a grown woman in the 'Cinderella' story. She questioned every tradition and pestered her aunt, Pushpa, whenever she mentioned Rahu and Ketu. She always wanted to understand the why, not just the what.

Once, when Clara Aunty told her the story of *Goldilocks and the Three Bears*, Sonali listened intently and then wrinkled her nose in confusion.

'But where do you find girls with golden hair?' she asked. 'I've never seen even one in our colony.'

Clara Aunty had laughed and brushed it off, but Sonali wasn't convinced. She scoured every classroom, every playground, and even peered into car windows at traffic signals, hoping to spot someone who fit the description.

When no golden-haired girl appeared, she returned to Clara Aunty days later and declared with quiet triumph, 'I think Goldilocks was made up.'

Clara Aunty had to rewrite the story, changing the character's name to Blackilocks to convince Sonali.

Sonali's world extended beyond places of worship and school corridors. It was stitched together with the hum of the fish market and the scent of freshly ground masalas wafting from either Chandra's vegetarian kitchen or Clara Aunty's non-vegetarian kitchen.

Festivals were a grand affair in the Nadkarni household. Christmas meant decorating the small plastic tree in Clara Aunty's living room, sneaking warm *kalkals* before they cooled, and staying past bedtime for Midnight Mass, feeling half-drowsy yet enchanted by the twinkling fairy lights. And Diwali? Diwali was magic. The house would glow with diyas, the kitchen would be filled with the scent of *besan laddus*, and the air would be thick with laughter and the smoke of firecrackers.

But despite this seamless blend, there were moments when she realised that not everyone saw the world the way she did.

For instance, a classmate wrinkled her nose at school and asked, 'Why do you drink that church water? Aren't you supposed to be a Hindu?'

Sonali blinked at her, utterly puzzled. Why was this even a question? Wasn't faith just another language? You could speak many languages without losing your own.

Only much later, when she moved to Mumbai for college, did she realise how rare her upbringing had been. Among new friends, she hesitated before crossing herself outside a church or stopping at a roadside temple. She felt the weight of labels—the boxes people wanted to put her in. But Sonali had never lived in boxes. She had always lived in spaces that flowed seamlessly into one another, where faith, friendship, and food were threads in the same fabric. She questioned every doubt and researched for answers until she was convinced. She thought beyond opinions. She felt in the realm where reality crystallised with facts.

She studied history and found that facts were prone to interpretation. She would spend hours in the college library, reading up on the day's lectures and finding conflicting opinions in books by different authors. She came prepared to the class the next day, armed with citations that contradicted each other. She was keen on uncovering the facts hidden beneath versions of the truth. She was argumentative with her professors about every historical fact, using her references, because she analysed deeply. She was a last-bencher, and her professors would often discuss her in the staff room. All faculty knew her, students knew her, and the books in the library were getting to know her.

And she intended to keep it that way.

Radhika

Radhika was never meant to be ordinary. Not the day she was born, not on the day she raced through the wheat fields faster than the village boys, and indeed not the day she rolled up her sleeves and marched into the family business of farming. But let's start at the beginning.

It was a muggy August night in Bada Gaon, where the air stuck to your skin. Inside the grand *haveli* of Chowdhary Harpal Singh, Sumitra Devi was in the throes of labour, her cries merging with the flickering of the brass diya near Gauri Ma's idol. Outside, a group of women sat, *odhnis* drawn low, whispering between fervent murmurs of '*Bhagwan kare, ladka ho!* (May God bless her with a boy!)' Then, finally, a wail pierced through the thick night air.

'*Chhori hoyi hai*, (It's a girl,)' the midwife announced flatly, and the dhols remained untouched, the prepared *laddus* mysteriously disappeared, and the atmosphere in the courtyard cooled several degrees. Harpal Singh's mother, *Daadima*, pursed her lips as if she had just bitten into a sour amla. The men in the *baithak* barely glanced up from their hookahs.

But inside the dimly lit room, Sumitra Devi looked at her daughter's scrunched-up face and whispered, '*Meri chhori toh chhoro se bhi tej niklegi*. (My daughter will outshine the boys.)'

And boy, was she right! They would know in due course of time.

Meanwhile, tradition had to be followed. The midwife massaged the baby's tiny limbs with warm mustard oil before wrapping her snugly in a soft, handwoven cloth. A few hours later, an iron *kada* was tied around the infant's delicate wrist to ward off the evil eye, and a small black *tikka* was placed behind her ear. That evening, the family gathered in the courtyard for the *Naam Karan*, though it was a quiet affair—no grand feast, no singing of auspicious songs. The village priest, an older man with a flowing white beard, dipped a mango leaf in a silver thali filled with Ganga Jal and touched it to the baby's lips.

'Radhika,' he announced, his voice carrying through the still air.

The name, chosen in reverence to Lord Krishna's beloved Radha, was met with approving nods from the elders, though the men barely glanced up from their hookahs. Sumitra, however, clutched her daughter protectively, silently vowing that one day, the world would celebrate her Radhika just as much as any son.

From the very beginning, Radhika was a little hurricane. She was always out in the fields, inspecting wheat crops with the same intensity as *Taiji* examined wedding proposals. She ran barefoot through the mustard fields, mud caked on her heels, her laughter rising above the village sounds like a bell. She was the only girl who could outplay the boys at *gilli danda* and outperform them on school tests, much to the surprise and dismay of the village elders.

It was clear that Radhika was no ordinary village girl. She had a sharp mind and an insatiable curiosity that set her apart. She could sit with the ladies, knead the dough, and embroider her *odhni*. She could sit with the boys, solving math problems faster than the schoolmaster could write on the blackboard. Radhika was one of the few girls in the village who attended school. *Daadima* believed that a girl's place was in the kitchen.

Sumitra insisted, '*Agar chhori padh le toh sasural mein izzat badh jave.* (If the girl gets educated, then her in-laws will respect her.)'

'The girl is like a sharp sword,' the village elders would mutter, watching her solve math problems on a slate while sitting on a charpai in the fields.

'And this sword will slit our throats someday,' Damyanti *Chachi* would add dramatically, conveniently ignoring that Radhika's sharp mind was winning the family more respect than they had ever imagined.

At home, she would pester her father with questions about the world beyond Bada Gaon, and at school, she aced every test. Her father, the stern and respected Chowdhary Harpal Singh, who once saw daughters as burdens, now swelled with pride whenever the schoolmaster came to praise his daughter.

'*Akhir chhori kiski hai?* (Whose daughter is she, afterall?)' he would declare, his voice laced with newfound respect, as the men in the *baithak* nodded in agreement.

One evening, as she sat on the charpai, working on her math problems, her father called her and gave her a mantra that would last forever.

'Fields are not just about crops, Radhika, they are about honour, too. Taking care of them is essential.'

His words stayed with her. The land was not just soil. It was their identity. She started to pay more attention to the conversations about farming. Being a quick learner, she soon advised the boys about the techniques. But as she grew older, her responsibilities at home increased. She learned to churn butter, make fresh rotis on the *chulha*, and manage the household accounts when her father was away.

'*Roti gol nahi bani, dobara bana*, (The chapati is not round, make it again,)' her mother corrected, her hands expertly flipping a perfectly round roti.

Despite her household duties, Radhika found solace in the fields. She loved the sound of the tubewell gushing water into the irrigation channels, peacocks dancing after the monsoon rains, and the scent of freshly harvested wheat. She felt an unspoken bond with the land.

Radhika was tall and broad-shouldered, carrying herself with easy confidence. Her skin was sun-kissed, a warm wheatish tone deepened by years under the Haryana sun. Her sharp, dark eyes held a steady gaze, constantly assessing, calculating, and missing nothing. A straight nose and full lips, often pressed into a thoughtful line, gave her face a striking sharpness—there was nothing delicate about Radhika, and she never pretended otherwise.

But of course, there was only one inevitable conclusion to a girl's story—marriage.

And so, at eighteen, Radhika found herself sitting stiffly in a marigold-draped courtyard, decked up in a heavily embroidered lehenga that weighed more than her ambitions. The *baraat* arrived with much fanfare, the dhols beating loudly this time because a wedding was a more worthy occasion for celebration than the birth of a daughter.

'Her in-laws are wealthy,' a woman whispered approvingly. 'I've heard that they are large landowners.'

Radhika sat through the ceremonies with a fixed smile, absorbing her mother's last-minute advice like a sponge.

'*Ghar ki izzat ka dhyan rakhna. Sasur ji ki izzat, pati ki seva—yeh hi ek aurat ka dharm hota hai.* (Take care of the family's reputation. Honouring your father-in-law, attending to your husband—that is the only duty of a woman.)'

But then, when Harpal Singh placed his hand on her head, he surprised her by saying, '*Apni akal ka bhi istemaal karna. Kisi se dabne ki zaroorat nahi.* (Use your head as well. There is no need to be suppressed by anyone.)'

Radhika met his gaze, her lips pressing together. '*Ji, Bauji*, (Yes, Father,)' she said quietly.

Her new home in Bahadurgarh was just as grand as her childhood *haveli*, but Radhika had no interest in sitting around in heavy jewellery and nodding dutifully at every instruction. By the end of the first week, she had rolled up her sleeves, marched straight into the fields, and started discussing soil quality with her father-in-law.

'*Yeh mitti thodi zyada ret wali hai,* (This mud has too much sand in it,)' she observed, rubbing a handful between her fingers.

Virender, her husband, was a traditionalist at heart.

Slightly bemused by his new wife's query, he raised an eyebrow. 'And you are a soil expert?'

'Since childhood,' she shot back, arms crossed. 'I understand farming, but I also understand family.'

That night, as she kneaded dough, Virender sipped his lassi and smirked. '*Bhai, tu toh nayi tarah ki bahu nikli.* (Man, you turned out to be a new kind of daughter-in-law.)'

Radhika smiled sweetly. 'Not new, just different.'

From that day forward, she was not just the bahu of the house but also her father-in-law's apprentice. She managed the household accounts better than the local shopkeepers, helped negotiate crop prices, and even dared to suggest new irrigation methods to her father-in-law, who, after much grumbling, had to admit that the new bahu knew her stuff.

The village women clucked their tongues, whispering about how Radhika walked the fields like a man. But Radhika didn't care.

Because she wasn't trying to be like a man.

Mona

Nestled in the folds of the Himalayas, Dehradun—or D'Doon, as teenagers affectionately called it—looked like it had stepped out of a postcard. The crisp, cool air, the scent of pine, and blooming flowers imparted a perpetual sense of freshness and rejuvenation to the town. D'Doon is dotted with colonial-era buildings, quaint cafes, bustling markets, and two of the most renowned boarding schools, one for girls and the other for boys.

Now, every town has its defining features. Paris has the Eiffel Tower. New York has yellow taxis. D'Doon? A Clock Tower. The Clock Tower that refused to tell the correct time but was somehow still the most punctual meeting point for budding romances.

The schools were the lifeblood of Dehradun, alongside the imposing Military Academy. The cadets, with their crisp, civil uniforms—dubbed 'muftis'—and crew cuts, sported an aura of mystery. Their chiselled features, sharp as their discipline, and deep tans made them seem almost unapproachable. They stuck together, a tight-knit group that never mingled with the locals. Even though the girls' school was just a stone's throw away and undeniably alluring, the cadets never strayed from their paths. Their discipline was their badge of honour.

These cadets were tantalising for the girls, eye candy with an edge. They'd gape, mouths slightly open, hearts fluttering, but the idea of making the first move was terrifying. The cadets, with their rigid training, were always out of reach.

But the boys from the neighbouring school? They were a different story. Eager and approachable, they were more than happy to befriend the girls. By the time students reached 10th or 11th grade, couples had already begun to form, and Saturday outings became the week's highlight. It was a time of stolen glances, secret smiles, and blossoming romances.

Among the parade of prim uniforms and polished shoes walked Mona—a glorious whirlwind in a pleated skirt, with eyes that sparkled like she'd swallowed the school's trophy cabinet. Head Girl. Debate Queen. Sprinter. The only girl who could pull off Shakespeare and a French plait simultaneously. And then there was Sandeep. Brooding. Tall. Mysteriously silent in a way that made him appear deep, though half the time he was just wondering whether or not he'd locked his dorm cupboard. A boy from a Rajput family so old-school that their dining room had more portraits than people.

Their first meeting wasn't on a Saturday town outing. It was at *The Masquerade Ball*—an annual event engineered to give hormonal teenagers an excuse to wear perfume and pretend they hadn't already stalked each other's class schedules.

The ballroom glittered like someone had shaken up a snow globe filled with sequins and teenage anxiety. Mona entered in a red gown that slowed time—or at least caused one boy to walk into a pillar. Her golden mask sparkled. Sandeep saw her and forgot how to breathe, speak, or form rational thoughts. He approached, his heart doing cartwheels.

'Can you guess who I am?' she teased.

'Those eyes,' he replied, very seriously, 'are unforgettable.'

They danced in the soft lighting and exchanged glances. The masks came off at midnight, but Mona and Sandeep had already been unmasked to each other.

Now, love in boarding school is a complicated affair. You have curfews, suspicious matrons, and 2.5 hours of freedom on Saturdays. However, that somehow made everything more cinematic. Their weekly escapades seemed inspired by a Netflix teen drama, although Netflix did not exist in the 1990s. Robber's Cave. Mussoorie drives. Long walks punctuated by dramatic sighs and philosophical questions like, 'What do you want to be when you grow up?' Answer: 'Yours.'

Their story was stitched together in moments—coffee spilt on a beloved copy of *Pride and Prejudice* ('You owe me a new Darcy,' she'd declared), secret notes slipped into lockers, and heated debates over poetry where passion occasionally overtook punctuation.

Mona was a force of nature—everywhere at once. She dominated the debating hall, sports field, theatre, and library. With long, wavy hair, bright almond eyes, and effortless charm, she was the school's queen bee—confident, clever, and magnetic.

Mona, a vibrant Sikh girl originally from Punjab and raised in the multicultural mosaic of Malaysia, was the daughter of a fiercely independent and affluent single mother. Her mother, Mohini Sidhu, was a self-made restaurateur with the spine of a lioness. She had raised Mona to be fearless, fabulous, and formidable.

'Never marry a man who can't cook,' she had warned.

Mona was accustomed to a cosmopolitan lifestyle where cultural and religious lines often blurred insignificantly.

Sandeep, on the other hand, was born in the heartland of Uttar Pradesh, in a sprawling ancestral *haveli* surrounded by lush fields and a community that revered his family. His upbringing was traditional, punctuated by rituals, festivals, and a deep reverence for heritage and lineage. His parents upheld Rajput pride and customs with unwavering devotion, grooming Sandeep to carry on this legacy. They sent him to an elite boarding school where the sons of royal families, industrialists, and film stars were refined in etiquette and style. Instead, he fell for a Sikh girl who quoted Virginia Woolf and wore mismatched socks.

When Mona and Sandeep first met, they were unaware of the weight of cultural complexities that lay ahead. Their love blossomed in stolen moments and whispered promises. Mona's laugh was a burst of sunshine in Sandeep's structured life, and his steadfast presence served as a grounding force in her whirlwind of activity. They navigated the rocky terrain of their disparate backgrounds with the unshakable belief that love could conquer all.

'You know, if my mom knew I was sneaking out with a zamindar's son, she'd have a fit,' Mona teased, her eyes twinkling with mischief as they sat under a tree, far from prying eyes.

'And if my father found out, he'd probably disown me,' Sandeep replied, though his smile was just as bright.

Their love blossomed like it always does at sixteen—recklessly, beautifully, with complete disregard for logic. They understood their parents would disapprove. They recognised that society would frown and probably have a collective aneurysm. But what teenager worth their salt lets logic interfere with romance?

Love, especially young love, is a peculiar thing. It makes you brave and foolish in equal measure. Mona and Sandeep knew the world outside would complicate things. But they were dreamers, adventurers, and rebels with a cause at the time. The future stretched beyond them, as vast and brilliant as the sky above. And for now, that was enough.

CHAPTER 2

Welcome to the USA

Sugandha

Sugandha folded a deep maroon Kanchi cotton sari. She placed it carefully in her suitcase, smoothing the edges with the efficiency she had honed over years of managing a household. The suitcase, a sturdy VIP model gifted by her husband, was already packed to the brim—ziplock pouches of home-ground masalas, neatly rolled cotton blouses, a small brass container of *kumkum*, and a vacuum-sealed bag of ghee-soaked sweets that her son used to devour as a child.

She paused, staring at the suitcase. America. Her son's world. So different from hers.

She had dreamed of this trip for years, imagining herself stepping off the plane and seeing Sharath waiting for her. Yet, now that it was happening, a tight knot of unease settled in her chest.

Would she fit in? Would her son still see her as his *Amma*? And more importantly, would he still be *her* Sharath—the one who needed just a whiff of sambhar to come running to the dining table?

'*Amma*, don't overpack,' Sharath had said over the phone, his voice laced with amused patience. 'You'll find everything here.'

Everything? Did they have the *right* kind of turmeric? The curd—would it taste the same? And what about filter coffee? Would it taste like coffee if not poured from a thin steel tumbler?

From the doorway, her mother, Rama, scoffed. 'You think they live in the jungle or what?'

Sugandha exhaled. 'You don't understand, *Amma*.'

'Oh, I understand *perfectly*,' Rama sniffed, crossing her arms like a well-seasoned war general. 'You'll go there, and that North Indian girl will have turned my grandson into someone I won't even recognise. Next thing you know, he'll start asking you for aloo paratha instead of *perugu annam*!'

Rama had spent years as the poised, peace-loving diplomat of the family, smoothing ruffled feathers and swallowing sharp words. But ever since Mr Reddy passed away a few years ago, she had developed a talent for expressing her thoughts, however bitter they might be.

Sugandha pressed her lips together. It's best to ignore that one.

From the living room, her husband's voice rang out. 'Passport? Tickets? All in the bag, no?'

'As if I'd forget,' she muttered, rolling her eyes.

A moment later, Satheesh stood beside her, adjusting his glasses. 'Just don't say anything about the girl when you go.'

She stiffened. Of course, she wasn't going to bring it up. But just the *thought* of it—of meeting *her*—made her uneasy. A North Indian girl. Not the daughter-in-law she had imagined, not the one she had mentally paired with Sharath over the years.

She turned to the wooden dresser, where a small, framed picture of Lord Venkateswara sat next to a well-thumbed copy of the

Hanuman Chalisa. Should she take a small idol for daily puja? Would her son think she was being *too much*?

Her fingers hovered over the frame, then withdrew. His voice always hesitated when she spoke of festivals, rituals, and tradition.

The apartment buzzed with last-minute activity. Satheesh checked his watch for the third time. Her mother muttered prayers, throwing in unsolicited travel advice in between.

'Drink some herbal tonic before the flight.'

'*Amma*, it's a *flight*, not a bus ride to Tirupati.'

Her nerves were stretched tight, but there was no time to dwell on them.

The driver honked from downstairs. It was time.

With a final glance around her home—the soft glow of the brass lamps in the puja room, the lingering scent of turmeric and incense—Sugandha stepped out. Her husband took the suitcase, her mother adjusted the pleats of her sari one last time, and she was on her way just like that.

The drive to the airport was mostly quiet, punctuated only by her husband's helpful reminders. 'Boarding pass—keep it handy. Don't put it inside the suitcase.'

She nodded absently, staring out of the window. Hyderabad had changed. The flyovers, the glass buildings, the neon signs—it wasn't the same city she had arrived in as a young bride. Back then, the roads were lined with hawkers calling out their wares, rickshaws rattling through narrow lanes, and the smell of street food mingling with fresh jasmine garlands.

The red-and-white barrier came down as they approached a railway crossing, halting traffic. A slow-moving train rumbled past, its carriages a blur in the dim evening light.

Sugandha's breath caught.

Machilipatnam.

The railway colony. A sixteen-year-old girl stood at the school gate, heart hammering, waiting for someone who had never returned.

A father whose silence crushed even the *idea* of love.

The train clattered past, disappearing into the distance. A sharp honk from behind snapped her back to the present. The barrier lifted, and traffic surged forward.

Sugandha gripped the edge of her sari. She was not that girl anymore.

The airport lights loomed ahead, bright and unrelenting.

Her stomach twisted. She had never been inside an airport before. She had never travelled so far from home.

Her husband exhaled, relieved. 'Not much traffic today.'

Sugandha's hands felt clammy. She adjusted her *pallu*, took a deep breath, and stepped out.

Debjyoti

Debjyoti Banerji was the woman who always carried a napkin, a safety pin, and a tiny tube of Boroline in her purse. She believed one of these three items could fix everything, whether a sudden emotional breakdown, a stubbornly loose button, or a scraped knee.

At 58, she possessed the elegance of an old Bengali painting—graceful, slightly faded around the edges, yet radiating a presence that filled the room. Her crisp, white Bengal cotton sari, with a thin red border, was always impeccably pleated. Her silver-streaked hair was twisted into a neat bun, and her round-rimmed glasses perched delicately on her nose. She exuded an air of quiet authority, with a soft yet firm voice akin to the first drizzle before a monsoon storm.

And yet, for all her poise, she was seated on a flight to Seattle, gripping the armrest like a lifeline.

'Oh, Ma Durga, this thing is shaking again!' she muttered, eyes shut tight. The American man in the seat next to her looked at her with concern.

'It's just turbulence, ma'am,' he said kindly.

Debjyoti gave him a tight smile. '*Baba*, this "just turbulence" is nothing but *badmash* air pockets. My younger daughter showed me on Google—very dangerous!'

The man blinked. He wasn't ready for a crash course in Bengali aerodynamics.

Debjyoti sighed and turned towards the tiny aeroplane window. She was going to Seattle to take care of her pregnant daughter, who, despite being a doctor herself, still called her mother twenty-seven times a day for things like 'Where is my purple dupatta?' or 'Ma, I forgot how to make *posto*, tell me na!'

She smiled despite herself. When the real *jhamela* began, she still needed her mother for all her modern American ways.

But underneath her calm exterior, Debjyoti was nervous.

She had been a sickly child—thin wrists, frail bones—but Shanta, her mother, always had a *Dabur Chawanprash* ready.

Debjyoti was nine when they cut her heart open.

It was 1975, and open-heart surgeries were still rare in India—a whispered miracle that only a few hospitals attempted. Barrackpore was no place for such medical feats, so Major Banerjee pulled every string, called in every favour, and wrote every letter until they secured a date at PGI Chandigarh. Six long years had passed since that terrifying day in Barrackpore when little Debu clutched her chest and collapsed, her tiny body betraying her in a way no child's should. Since then, life had been a blur of hospital corridors, waiting rooms, and doctors who spoke in complicated terms while her parents nodded gravely.

Shanta had been a quiet strength throughout her entire journey. She sat ramrod straight as they went to the hospital to prepare for the surgery. She didn't cry, wail, or let anyone see the terror pooling in her eyes. Instead, she fed Debjyoti small bites of *luchi* and *aloo dom* as if stuffing her child with love in food might fortify her for what was to come.

Debjyoti, of course, didn't understand the fuss. She had never felt particularly sick, only slightly tired compared to the other kids. No one had let her run or climb, but she had books, her *Baba's* stories, and *misti doi* on Sundays. That was enough. But then, she had overheard a nurse whispering to another, using words like 'risky' and 'critical'.

And for the first time, she was afraid.

The night before the surgery, her father sat by her bedside. Major Bannerji was not a man of many words—his love was in the steadying hand on her shoulder, in the way he always carried her when she was tired, in the way he had fought to bring her here. He cleared his throat.

'You know, when I was a cadet, I had a friend—Jaspreet,' he began, rubbing his thumb absentmindedly over the brass buckle of his belt. 'He had a scar right here.' He pointed to his chest. 'Shrapnel wound. People used to call him "*Fauji* with a broken heart".'

Debjyoti giggled. 'Did he survive?'

'Of course,' Baba said gruffly. 'Became one of the best officers in the unit. Used to say his heart was patched up but stronger for it.'

She stared at him. 'Will mine be stronger, too?'

Major Banerjee's face softened, and he touched her forehead gently. 'Stronger than all of us.'

The surgery was six hours long.

Six hours of waiting in a sterile hospital corridor, of Shanta gripping her husband's hand so hard her nails dug into his skin. She hadn't prayed so fervently since the war.

When the doctor emerged, sweat beading his forehead, he removed his mask and said, 'She's a fighter.'

Shanta burst into tears then, silently gasping, sobbing into her *anchal*, her whole body shaking with relief. Major Bannerji, ever the soldier, only nodded sharply, jaw tightening. But later that night, he let his shoulders slump when he sat alone outside the hospital room with a cigarette in one hand and a trembling cup of chai in the other.

His little girl had come back to him.

When Debjyoti woke up, her chest ached as if someone had stolen a piece of her and stitched it back differently. Her *Baba* sat beside her, pretending to read the newspaper, while Ma hovered, adjusting pillows and stroking her hair. A white and firm bandage ran down her front.

'*Baba*,' she croaked, voice hoarse from the anaesthesia.

He looked up.

'I'll have a scar like your friend, Jaspreet.'

For the first time in days, her father laughed. Not just a chuckle but a full-bodied, relieved, grateful laugh.

He leaned over, kissed her forehead, and whispered, 'Yes, *beta.* You will.'

Years later, whenever Debjyoti traced the thin silver scar on her chest, she didn't think of the fear or the pain. She thought of her mother's trembling hands feeding her *luchi*, her father's stories, and the moment she returned to them.

Her patched heart had carried her through everything since. And yes, she liked to believe it was stronger for it.

An old fear gnawed at her as she prepared to become a grandmother. Was this thing hereditary? Was it sleeping somewhere in her blood, waiting to pass on? She had been terrified when she had her daughters, obsessively checking their medical reports. And now, here she was again, hovering over her unborn grandchild like a paranoid hawk.

'Ma, you'll be fine!' her younger daughter, Pari, said on the phone before she boarded the flight. 'Please don't go full on on *Didi* with your lectures.'

'I never lecture!' Debjyoti had huffed.

Pari had snorted. '*Haan haan*, you only *gently* remind us a thousand times.'

Now, the aircraft gave another lurch, and Debjyoti gasped. The American man awkwardly patted her hand. 'Maybe some water?'

She nodded, embarrassed. '*Baba*, do you have whiskey?'

The man burst out laughing, and so did she.

When she landed, her daughter, Supriya, was already waiting for her at the airport, with swollen feet in chappals and waving furiously.

'Ma! You're here!'

As she waddled towards her, Debjyoti felt the old fears settle in her bones again. She had been carrying them for so long, like invisible luggage. She reached for her daughter's hand and squeezed it gently.

'Come, *baba*, let's go home. I'll make you some *shukto*.'

Because that's what you did, right? When you didn't have the answers, when you couldn't control fate, when old fears still lurked in your heart, you fed the people you loved, wrapped them in warmth, and hoped that was enough.

Maybe it was.

Sonali

As Sonali zipped up her suitcase, her mind was still half occupied with the end-of-semester papers she had graded earlier that day. She had spent years teaching students about the past, analysing empires, revolutions, and shifting cultural landscapes. Every summer, during vacation, she had the chance to visit a destination of historical importance. However, this year, she was visiting Seattle, visiting Aman.

Across the room, Rajesh was sifting through a pile of documents, muttering under his breath about misplaced boarding passes.

'Rajesh, I sent you the tickets by email. Just check your phone,' she reminded him, folding her reading glasses into her handbag.

'Paper tickets feel more reliable,' he grumbled, adjusting his glasses.

Sonali sighed. For a man who had spent his career in engineering, Rajesh was hopelessly old-school when it came to travel. On the other hand, she had spent years adapting to new ideas and perspectives.

She was visiting her son, Aman, to understand the world he had built and the choices he had made. She had spent a lifetime studying societal shifts, yet the one happening in her home—the one that had quietly unsettled her—felt more complex to decode.

Would Aman be different now?

She glanced at her bookshelf one last time before heading out. A well-worn copy of *A History of Changing Societies* sat wedged between biographies of forgotten queens and political theorists.

Change was inevitable. She had taught that lesson a hundred times.

Now, it was time to live it, and it's easier said than done!

Sonali sat stiff-backed and mildly annoyed in the middle seat of the aircraft's middle row. It was a long-haul flight—Mumbai to Seattle, with a layover in Frankfurt. Her left shoulder ached, her right thigh was cramped, and her personal space had been unceremoniously annexed by the woman next to her, a large, affable lady who had spread out comfortably, claiming the armrest as if it were her birthright.

Sonali shot her a tight, polite smile. The lady beamed back.

Sonali sighed inwardly. The middle seat was a no-man's land, a diplomatic neutral zone where conversations were brief, friendships unlikely, and shifting for comfort was an ongoing, unwinnable battle.

She turned to the other side. Rajesh was fast asleep. Of course, he was. His head lolled slightly to the side, earphones in place, eyes shut in blissful unconsciousness. The steady hum of the aircraft was nothing less than a lullaby for him.

'Unbelievable,' she muttered.

Rajesh could fall asleep anywhere. He slept before the aircraft took off, the train left the platform, and a bus started rolling. Unlike Sonali, who carried the weight of a thousand unfinished thoughts into the night, he had perfected the art of shutting down his thoughts.

She turned back and shifted a little, careful not to jostle the lady beside her, who had now dozed off, her elbow still firmly on the armrest. There was something deeply symbolic about this, Sonali thought. The middle of the row, the middle seat, mid-air, and—let's face it—the middle of life.

Middle age. That strange limbo where youth had faded, but old age had not quite arrived. The silver strands had started weaving through her hair, and the laughter lines had settled, making her look permanently serious, even when she wasn't. Not that she minded looking serious. She was a professor, after all. A professor of history. It suited her. What didn't suit her was this increasing feeling of being... caught. Between generations. Between ideas. Between what was and what was to come.

She glanced at Rajesh again. He was the quintessential middle child—an expert negotiator, peacemaker, observer. He had spent his entire childhood balancing an elder sibling's expectations and a younger one's indulgences. It had made him level-headed, accommodating, and deeply, profoundly absent-minded.

'Rajesh,' she whispered, nudging him slightly.

Nothing.

She jabbed him harder.

'Huh?' He blinked groggily.

'Water. Can you get me some?'

He peered blearily around, then pressed the call button without sitting up.

'*Arre*, why did you wake me up?'

'I need water.'

'You should have woken me up when they were serving drinks.'

'They serve drinks?' she asked, surprised.

'Yes, I think so.'

'When?'

'Maybe Frankfurt? Or before?' He rubbed his eyes. 'Anyway, what's the time?'

'We are on a plane, Rajesh. Time is relative.'

The air hostess arrived, already holding a bottle of water. Rajesh smiled a charming smile at her, thanking her as he handed the bottle to Sonali. 'Here you go.'

Sonali took it without responding. The man could be exasperating. But then, she could have pressed the button and called for water herself! She could be exasperating as well!

She tried to sleep but failed, her mind now meandering into her profession. Teaching history had been her life's work, but it was changing. The students were different now. They studied for exams, not for the sake of knowledge. They chose courses based on earning potential, rather than their curiosity.

'Like my own son,' she thought with an uneasy pang.

Aman had always been brilliant. Thoughtful and perceptive, yet he had chosen economics. A field that promised a stable future, a good salary, and security. Nothing wrong with that. And yet, a part of her longed for him to have chosen differently, to have studied something purely for love. But who was she to judge? Hadn't she encouraged him towards the best opportunities?

She shifted again. This seat was a conspiracy against the spine.

Next time, she decided firmly, Business Class.

She had read somewhere that it would manifest in reality if you could imagine something enough. She closed her eyes and pictured herself reclining in one of those plush seats, sipping warm tea, and stretching her legs luxuriously. Her bobbed hair was always impeccable and needed minimal brushing. 'Wish everything in life could be tamed as easily,' she thought as she ran her hand through her hair.

The aircraft hummed on, soaring over unknown lands and endless seas, and Sonali drifted into a dream somewhere between wakefulness and sleep, between past and future.

She dreamt she had arrived in Seattle. Aman was at the airport, his familiar, lanky frame leaning casually against a pillar, waiting for her. She smiled in her sleep, and in that moment, even the middle seat didn't seem so bad.

Radhika

Radhika stood on the balcony of her farmhouse, gazing out at the vast expanse of land that stretched beyond the horizon. Neat rows of golden wheat swayed under the setting sun, resulting from decades of toil and transformation. What had once been a collection of fragmented ancestral fields was now a thriving agribusiness empire. She expanded the family's farming operations beyond traditional crops, introducing modern irrigation, high-yielding seeds, and even organic farming to cater to the growing demands of international markets.

She was no longer just a village woman managing her husband's fields—she was Radhika Devi, the undisputed matriarch of Haryana's agricultural elite. Traders, politicians, and industry leaders sought her time, and newspapers hailed her as a woman who had revolutionised farming in North India. She built warehouses, started food processing units, and collaborated with global firms. From the bustling mandi to international trade fairs, her name commanded respect.

She turned to stand before the photograph of her mother, Sumitra Devi. The black-and-white image stared back at her, a woman of quiet strength, her eyes full of stories Radhika had lived to fulfil. A lump rose in her throat.

She bowed her head, the weight of decades pressing down on her shoulders, and whispered, voice thick with unshed tears:

'*Thari chhori ne thaari laaj raakhi, Maa.* (Your daughter has upheld your honour, Ma.)'

Her mother's gaze didn't change, and the photograph remained still. However, deep in her heart, Radhika swore she could feel the slightest nod of approval.

Radhika wore a traditional salwar kameez that reflected her roots. The vivid, vibrant colours echoed her bold personality, and her long hair was neatly plaited, just as it had been in her youth. At 68, Radhika had jet-black hair, and people found it hard to believe she had never used hair dye. Simple yet elegant jewellery adorned her wrists and ears, a sign of her deep cultural pride. To the villagers, she represented strength, tradition, and progress.

Yet, none of this mattered if her son wasn't there to inherit it.

Her son, Vikram, had gone abroad to study at the Centre for Sustainable Global Enterprise at Cornell, just as she had planned. After working at various companies, he joined the Bill & Melinda Gates Foundation in Seattle as a senior program officer for Nutritious Food Systems. Radhika had imagined him returning with qualifications and modern knowledge, ready to elevate their empire. But that was twenty years ago. Vikram had built a life in America with little space for wheat fields and village politics. He visited for short holidays, talked about his work in detached tones, and never stayed long enough to see what she had created for him.

When Vikram was a little boy, Radhika recalled him running through the fields with a toy tractor, declaring that he would grow the best wheat in the village. She had smiled then, believing those words. But now, she feared they had been just the fleeting dreams of a child.

Both Radhika and Vikram received excellent education in agriculture. While she understood the land through intuition and experience, he specialised in data, automation, and precision farming. His world involved satellites mapping crop yields, AI-driven irrigation systems, and sustainable food production. He collaborated with global firms to develop farming solutions that boost productivity while reducing manual labour. For him, the future of agriculture depended on automation rather than human hands working the soil.

Radhika turned to her assistant, Mahendra, who had been with her since the early days of her journey. He stood respectfully by the doorway, waiting for instructions.

'Madamji, the delegates from Delhi have arrived. They're waiting in the hall,' he informed her.

Radhika exhaled sharply. 'Let them wait. I need to finish this call first.'

She picked up the landline and dialled Vikram's number. It was morning in Seattle, and she knew he would be rushing to work. The phone rang twice before he answered.

'Ma? Everything okay?' His voice was brisk and efficient.

'Everything is fine, *beta*,' she said, her tone controlled. 'When are you coming home?'

'Ma, we talked about this.... I have work. Maybe next year.'

Radhika's grip on the phone tightened. 'Next year, next year.... You always say next year, Vikram. Do you even know what I have built here? What is waiting for you?' She wanted to scream on the phone, but softened her tone and said, 'Come for at least a few weeks. We'll talk. You'll see what I've done.'

There was a brief silence on the other end. Then Vikram said, 'Ma... I can't make any promises. My work—it's different from what you're doing. I'm helping farmers but in a new way. It's not about owning land anymore, Ma. It's about technology and efficiency. The future isn't in ploughing fields, Ma. It's in making farming smarter.'

Radhika closed her eyes and took a deep breath. She thought of her father, her husband, and the generations who had nurtured this land before her. *What is farming without the farmer? What is land if not owned, loved, and nurtured?*

Enough waiting. Enough asking. With a determined glint in her eyes, she straightened her dupatta, adjusted the gold bangles on her wrist, and strode down the marble staircase for her meeting with the delegates from Delhi.

As she descended, her heels clicked against the cool stone, echoing through the grand hall. Lining the walls were generations of men—her ancestors—frozen in sepia, their moustaches thick, their gazes stern, a parade of patriarchy, each more formidable than the last. And yet, she was standing taller than all of them, not in a photograph but in flesh and blood, running an empire they could never have imagined.

She paused at the doorway, turned to Mahendra, and with a flick of her dupatta, declared:

'*Mahendra,* Seattle *ka* ticket *katwa de.* First class. *Main apne chhore ne ghar le aavan ja ri.* (Mahendra, get me a ticket to Seattle. First class. I'm going to bring my son home.)'

It was time to bring her son home.

Mona

When Sandeep announced he was marrying Mona many years later, his Rajput family reacted like he'd declared war on their lineage.

His father thundered, 'A Sikh girl from Malaysia? *Beta*, what will she even cook?'

His grandmother let out a deep sigh that could stir their ancestors, while his mother muttered darkly, 'Not married till he's married.'

Meanwhile, in Malaysia, Mona's mother sipped her chai and sighed. 'A Thakur from Uttar Pradesh? *Wah beta*, why not just jump into a Bollywood movie?'

The engagement was a battlefield of polite hostilities. Mona, breezing into Sandeep's ancestral *haveli* in a perfectly respectable suit, was met with stares sharp enough to cut glass.

'She wears sleeveless?' one aunt whispered.

'She drinks wine?' another gasped.

But the real earthquake hit at dinner.

'*Beta*, have some more ghee,' Sandeep's mother said sweetly, piling her plate high.

Mona took a cautious bite. 'This is amazing! But I might need to run a marathon after this.'

The room fell silent. Even the kachoris on her plate seemed to freeze.

Sandeep kicked her under the table. 'They don't joke about ghee here.'

Despite the whispers, Mona stood firm. She learned to drape a sari, attended pujas, and even mastered the art of nodding during lengthy discussions over land disputes. The ice finally broke when Sandeep's mother found her in the kitchen, stirring a pot with urgency.

'You're making halva?'

Mona wiped flour off her face. 'Yes, Aunty. And please tell me if this looks okay.'

For the first time, Sandeep's mother smiled. 'You need more ghee.'

The wedding was a spectacular mix of turbaned *baraatis*, bhangra dancers, and bewildered relatives.

Mona walked around the fire in her crimson lehenga and whispered to Sandeep, 'Why seven times? Feels excessive.'

He smirked. 'You're marrying into my *khaandaan*, Mona. Seven rounds are the least of your worries.'

She squeezed his hand. 'We did it.'

Sandeep grinned. 'This is just the beginning.'

And with that, they dove headfirst into their happily-ever-after—armed with love, humour, and a lifetime supply of ghee.

Caste, class, and social status seemed trivial compared to what lay ahead. Over time, Mona and Sandeep's marriage, once a rebellious inter-caste and intercontinental love saga, gradually unravelled. After 19 years, Sandeep, now a comfortably middle-aged man who still considered himself God's gift to women, strayed. In his midlife foolishness, he became involved with a bright-eyed intern who was half his age and twice as gullible at the office.

'Don't be dramatic, Mona,' Sandeep had scoffed, stuffing his laptop into his bag like a man with nothing to hide. 'You're blowing this out of proportion. I was just talking to her.'

Mona raised an eyebrow, arms crossed. 'Oh, of course. Just talking. And what exactly does "You looked so pretty in that red dress today, sweetheart" mean?'

Sandeep rolled his eyes. 'It's called being nice, Mona. You should try it sometime.'

Mona let out a sharp laugh. 'Right. Being "nice" is what we're calling it now. Do you also "*nicely*" book hotel rooms for these conversations?'

He sighed, exasperated. 'Why are you so bitter?'

'Oh, I don't know, Sandeep. Maybe because my husband has the romantic maturity of a college fresher?'

He slammed his bag shut. 'You've never trusted me.'

'No, I did. A long time ago. Before I learned better.'

And just like that, they were done. Not legally, not officially. But in every way that mattered.

Mona, shattered but not foolish, stayed—not for some noble martyr act—because she refused to let Sandeep's midlife crisis wreck her daughter's future. And oh, what a crisis it was! Over time, Sandeep shifted from one pathetic office fling to a full-blown Internet Casanova, chatting up random women like a lonely uncle at a wedding. He managed to keep his business running and earn enough money to sustain Mona's luxurious lifestyle. This was a deal Mona had to accept. Mona also worked tirelessly at her small café in the upscale and posh Khan Market, ensuring that her daughter, Nitya, whom she affectionately called Neetu, received the education, exposure, and life she deserved. Finally, she sent Neetu off to the US—far, far away from her father's man-child nonsense.

Mona had always radiated effortless elegance since her school days. Now, at 48, she is consistently impeccably dressed in luxury designer clothing, carrying herself with the poise of someone who recognises her worth. Every aspect of her appearance is carefully curated—her hair is styled flawlessly, her nails are always manicured, and her jewellery is subtle yet clearly luxurious. Confident and assertive, Mona moves through the world with sophistication, never hesitating to share her opinions. Though accustomed to privilege, she is sharp, resourceful, and unafraid to take charge when needed. With a deep appreciation for art, culture, and fine dining, she enjoys life's finer pleasures but reserves her fiercest passion for her daughter.

Mona planned to visit Neetu in Seattle, where she studied at the University of Washington. Mona was a seasoned traveller who had travelled abroad on many occasions. Just last year, she visited Seattle to assist Neetu with her admission process. She knew airport lounges better than her kitchen, could sniff out a duty-free deal from a mile away, and her credit card limit could fund a small island nation.

This trip was a mission. Mona had been worried about Nitya. She felt it was her responsibility to ensure that her daughter wasn't doing anything foolish, like falling for the first charming idiot who came along. Of course, there will be shopping, perhaps some art galleries, and a Michelin-starred meal. A little indulgence never hurt anyone.

The difference on this trip was that Mona wasn't the one setting the rules. She would enter Neetu's world, which might not have room for her designer handbags or her well-meaning but slightly overbearing, maternal concerns. But that's for another day.

CHAPTER 3

Five Separate Journeys

Sugandha

In the tiny living room of Sharath's small apartment in Bellevue, Sugandha's world seemed to shrink. The scene outside unfolded like a postcard. The city skyline stretched toward the sky, a mix of glass towers reflecting the shifting hues of dusk. Beyond the clusters of high-rises, the snow-capped peaks of the Cascades stood tall, their outlines softened by the evening haze.

Down below, the streets pulsed with quiet energy—Tesla after Tesla glided past, their near-silent hum blending with the occasional honk of a hurried commuter. A group of young tech professionals, coffee cups in hand, walked briskly toward a modern café, engaged in animated conversation. A cyclist zipped by in the dedicated bike lane, dodging a pedestrian lost in their phone.

In the distance, Meydenbauer Bay shimmered under the setting sun, sailboats bobbing gently on the calm waters. The lakeside park was speckled with joggers and families enjoying the crisp Pacific

Northwest air. A woman, wrapped in a puffer jacket, sipped her coffee while her golden retriever eagerly watched a flock of ducks paddling near the shore.

Inside the apartment, the warmth of yellow lights contrasted with the cool tones of the evening outside. A faint aroma of freshly brewed coffee lingered in the air, blending with the soft hum of a robotic vacuum gliding across the hardwood floor.

Sugandha stood there, hands on her hips, staring at the whirring, blinking, utterly smug-looking contraption zipping around as if it owned the place. It was a sleek, silver, sci-fi-like disc that moved about with great purpose, gobbling up dust and debris as if on a mission from NASA. '*Aiyyo*, what is this space-age *kondaru*?!' she muttered.

Since she had landed in Seattle, Sugandha took it upon herself to whip the household into shape. Cooking, cleaning, and ensuring her son, Sharath, ate something other than bagels and Chipotle were her sacred duties as an Indian mother. Back home, she was the undisputed queen of domestic efficiency, reigning over an army of maids who dusted, swept, scrubbed, and polished every surface to perfection. But this American style of housework? *Aiyyo!* Robots instead of maids!

Sharath's beautiful home was all cool blue and elegant grey, with tasteful little potted plants in every corner. 'Too much dusting,' Sugandha thought. 'This would never work in India. One storm, and the entire house would look like it had been dipped in atta!'

As the cleaning marvel twirled around the coffee table, Sugandha's mind drifted back to India, to Anamma, their ever-cheerful housemaid, whose loud, dramatic sighs and off-tune songs were as much a part of their household as the furniture. Anamma would stomp about with a broom, pausing only to deliver wisdom on everything from politics to pickles. 'A robot!' Sugandha thought, 'Pah! This thing doesn't even complain about back pain! Where's the fun in that?'

With a chuckle, she leaned against the kitchen counter, watching the bot's determined little pirouettes. 'I wonder if it takes tea breaks,' she mused. 'Or if it prefers chai or coffee.' Anamma, of course, was a staunch supporter of strong, syrupy *kaapi* and would firmly refuse any nonsense about green tea or even regular chai.

In their bustling colony in Hyderabad, maids were the keepers of secrets, the first responders to crises, and the most reliable source of breaking news. Anamma, for example, always knew which daughter-in-law had stomped off to her mother's house, which family was buying gold, and who had sneakily watered down the milk packets before selling them. This robot, efficient as it was, had no idea how to conduct an afternoon gossip session while chopping beans at lightning speed.

A ping from her phone snapped her out of her thoughts. It was a message from her friend, Rupa, in India, eager to hear about her adventures in the land of DIY living. Sugandha quickly typed back about her new automated cleaning companion.

The reply was instant: '*Aiyyo*, if that thing can fold clothes and make round dosas, then pack one for me also!'

Sugandha burst out laughing, her eyes crinkling in delight.

She thought as she typed, 'This robot may be the future, but it'll never match the drama, humour, and sheer inefficiency of Anamma.'

In the meantime, with great self-importance, the cleaning bot let out a triumphant beep and trundled off to its charging station.

'Mission accomplished!' Sharath declared, stepping into the kitchen with a grin.

'Aah, Ram Ram!' Sugandha folded her hands mock-seriously at the retreating bot. 'Off it goes to report to the electric board about its victories over dust and filth.'

Sharath shook his head, laughing. '*Amma*, you and your imagination!'

But that's how she had always been—keen observer, meticulous planner, and careful talker.

Right then, she surveyed the spotless living room. That day was a special cleaning spree, a preparation. She was gearing up to meet Sharath's North Indian girlfriend, and if first impressions were anything to go by, a sparkling clean apartment was non-negotiable. Not that she had anything against the girl personally (yet), but a mother had to assert some quiet dominance, no? A spotless home, the scent of freshly made filter coffee, and a subtle display of her Lord Venkateswara idol—just a few gentle reminders that culture ran deep in this household. Cleaning was complete, and Sugandha had bigger things to tackle, like figuring out how to charm, assess, and, if necessary, outwit the new woman in her son's life.

The meeting was set for that evening. Sheena lived in the same apartment building. 'She is used to walking in and out of Sharath's apartment,' Sugandha thought, and before she could continue to overthink, the doorbell rang.

Sugandha adjusted the *pallu* of her neatly draped cotton sari, smoothed the pleats, and took a deep breath. Her gold *jhumkas* swayed as she moved, the only sign of nervous energy she allowed herself to show. Sharath smiled as he walked up to the door. He opened it with a flourish and invited Sheena into the house with an exaggerated bow!

And then—Sheena entered!

Resplendent in a neon green top that could blind satellites and a shiny pink skirt that likely had its own gravitational pull, she stood in stark contrast to Sugandha's muted world, like a dazzling tropical bird in an Arctic landscape. Her metal bangles jingled as she leaned in for an enthusiastic hug.

'Aunty! I've been *dying* to meet you!' Sheena beamed, her eyes alight with excitement.

Sugandha stiffened slightly, then gave a polite nod. 'Come in, *beta*.'

Sheena flounced inside, taking in the brass idols, the neatly folded prayer shawl, and the meticulously arranged spice boxes on the kitchen counter. 'Oh wow, Aunty! You have made the home smell *exactly* like an Indian temple.'

She laughed, scrunching her nose playfully, unaware of the slight stiffening of Sugandha's shoulders.

Sugandha smiled—just barely. She wasn't sure if it was meant as a compliment.

Would Sheena ever understand that this scent, this space, was not just an aesthetic but a way of life?

She didn't have to wait too long for the answer. It came sandwiched between mouthfuls of *pulihora* that Sugandha had prepared, and Sheena loved every bit of it.

'Shouldn't we take Aunty to the *Garba* night?' Sheena asked Sharath as she added another serving to her plate. 'It's right there in the park. I'm sure we'll have fun!'

If you've ever lived in the warmer corners of the Indian diaspora, you'll know that they don't just celebrate festivals. They throw out entire wardrobes, *dabbas* full of food, and deep-seated nostalgia at them. Navratri was that memory of India in the charming patch of Seattle that Sharath now called home—colourful, dramatic, and impossible to ignore. They joined the gathering that evening.

The park where Sugandha took her daily walks had undergone a transformation almost overnight. The same bench where she once sat with a flask of coffee and watched toddlers argue over sand toys was now within drumbeat distance of a full-blown *Garba* ground. Food stalls sprouted like mushrooms, filling the air with the seductive scents of *chole*, *pav bhaji*, and samosas....

The dancers had arrived in full festive splendour—*ghagras* spun like candy tops, and dupattas billowed in the breeze. The dhol beats and disco lights blurred all the cultural distinctions. Gujarati,

Telugu, Marathi, Punjabi—everyone swirled in unison like one large, spinning Indian ethos.

Sugandha, in the middle of it all, mused silently. 'Festivals unite Indians the way the Indian store does—everyone comes looking for something familiar and leaves with ten other things they didn't need but couldn't resist.'

Sheena's gang of twenty-somethings bounced around enthusiastically. Sheena was draped in a half-sari that made her look like an influencer among other girls.

'*Chole bhature* or *pav bhaji*?' Sheena asked, eyes gleaming at the food stalls.

'*Pav bhaji*,' Sharath said instantly, knowing it was Sheena's favourite. He smiled like a man who had just played the right card in a never-ending game of relationship poker.

Sugandha found herself bonding with another woman in a silk sari. 'Isn't the energy here just amazing?' she said, handing over her coupon for jalebis.

'Absolutely! I'm from Hyderabad, and this is my first *Garba* night!' the woman replied, grinning.

'*Aiyyo*! I am also from Hyderabad, and this is my first *Garba* night!' exclaimed Sugandha gleefully.

Within moments, they were in rapid-fire Telugu, comparing local bakeries, family dentists, and weather tantrums from their hometown.

On the sidelines, teenagers were perfecting spins they had just learnt from YouTube. *Dandiyas* clicked, phones recorded, and someone screamed, 'Brooo, that was lit!'—possibly about a dance move, or the samosa.

As the evening melted into night, Sugandha noticed something. Beneath the sequins and sparkle, there was a quiet truth wrapped in the laughter and swirling skirts—these young ones, so light on their feet, were also light on their roots. They would move, shift, and fly, from small towns to big cities, from internships to corporations. She watched Sheena and Sharath share a plate of *pav bhaji*, laughing at a private joke that only exists between people who have built a home inside each other.

And suddenly, she understood something that was not written in any immigration handbook. Home isn't always a place. Sometimes it's a borrowed dupatta, a well-timed joke, or a shared Netflix password. It's what you carry when you've left everything else behind.

Watching them twirl to a Gujarati beat under a Seattle sky, Sugandha smiled.

Maybe Sharath was learning to build his home, too.

Debjyoti

On a bright, breezy Saturday morning, Supriya dragged Debjyoti out for a 'must-do' mission. 'First stop—Indian store! We have two nearby, can you believe it? They stock everything—like a proper bazaar back home!' she grinned.

Debjyoti, still getting used to America, stepped inside and was instantly hit by a wave of nostalgia. '*Arrey Baap re*! (Oh my God!) Look at all this!' she gasped, her eyes flitting from shelves bursting with garam masala to stacks of Haldiram's sweets. Someone had crammed the entire subcontinent into four walls and a cash counter.

The store, nestled between a yoga studio and a Mexican taqueria, was a chaotic, glorious, full-bodied experience of Bharat in miniature. The aroma of *hing* and *elaichi* mingled in the air, Bollywood hits played softly in the background, and customers navigated the narrow aisles like autos in Delhi traffic—swift, ruthless, and unbothered by personal space.

'Ma, it's like all of India is here in one tiny shop!' Supriya chirped, picking up a pack of frozen parathas.

Debjyoti nodded, a bemused smile on her face. 'The things I am seeing here, we don't get in our stores in Kolkata! This is the real Unity in Diversity!' she mused.

As they strolled through the aisles, Debjyoti couldn't help but feel a prickle of worry for Supriya. The girl was five months pregnant, for heaven's sake! Yet here she was, running around, grocery shopping, cooking, doing laundry, handling work calls, and fixing that pesky leaking tap. Back home in Kolkata, she'd have been treated like a delicate *mishti doi ka bartan* (dish of sweet yoghurt), handled with the utmost care, with her feet propped up, pampered with coconut water and *laddus* by a battalion of well-meaning *kakimas* and *mashis*. But here, in this cold, efficient America, no one fussed over expectant mothers the way they should.

Debjyoti's brow knitted together. '*Eto mehnat korchish keno* (Why are you working so hard), Supriya? Just order online, no?' she muttered.

Supriya, of course, just grinned and kept tossing things into the trolley. 'I am going to do this myself from now on,' thought Debjyoti as she planned menus in her mind.

The sheer variety left her floored. God's idols sat next to Maggi packets. Fresh *karela* lay beside frozen samosas. In one corner, a group of aunties intensely discussed which brand of ready-to-eat *khichdi* most closely resembled home.

Debjyoti, newly arrived from Kolkata, was more intrigued by another aspect—Americans and their enthusiastic greetings. Back home, people stared openly, but casual hellos? *Na baba!* Smiling at strangers could earn you a '*Ki holo, pagol hoye gechho?* (What happened? Have you gone mad?)' Here, though, greetings were flying left, right, and centre.

The cashier, a lively young woman in a salwar kameez, chirped, 'How are you today?'

Supriya replied easily, 'Good, thanks! How about you?'

Debjyoti decided to try this newfound friendliness. Spying a fellow shopper—a bespectacled Bengali gentleman inspecting mustard oil bottles—she flashed her brightest smile and said, 'Hi!'

Uncle looked at her like she'd asked him to hand over his bank PIN.

Hmph. So much for cultural assimilation.

As she walked away, slightly crestfallen, she turned to Supriya. 'This is odd. Americans greet everyone, but we Indians behave like we're all on some top-secret mission, avoiding each other's eyes!'

Supriya laughed. 'Ma, it's not that simple! Although we may appear the same to Americans, we are aware of our differences, no? All Indians have different fields of expertise. South Indians dominate the tech industry, Punjabis own half the gas stations, Gujaratis are running motels—everyone finds their own tribe here! We might not all say hello, but come Independence Day, every Indian in town will turn up in full *josh*—tricolour dupattas, loud dhol beats, and emotional "Vande Mataram" sing-alongs!'

Debjyoti thought about it and smiled. They were in America, but they were still hoarding Everest masalas, sending kids to *Bharatnatyam* classes, and finding ways to be more Indian than India itself.

'Maybe,' she mused, 'if you ever want to see the "United States of India", head to the nearest Indian store. It's worth the trip—aisle to aisle, state to state, with a little bit of home tucked into every shelf.'

As they returned to the car, Debjyoti fussed over the shopping bags like an overprotective hen. 'Give me that,' she insisted, trying to pile all the bags onto herself, gasping as she loaded them into the boot.

Meanwhile, Supriya, as cool as *Shosha*, slid into the driver's seat, adjusting the rearview mirror, smiling, and watching her mother huffing and puffing.

Debjyoti clicked her tongue in disapproval. '*Eto bojha tolar ki dorkar* (Is it necessary to lift this burden)? You're five months pregnant, not training for the Olympics!' she scolded, wiping imaginary sweat off her forehead.

Supriya just chuckled, waving her off.

But Debjyoti wasn't convinced. '*Aakash ke bola uchit—ekla jete debe na*! (Aakash should be told—don't let her go alone!)' she muttered under her breath.

If the boy had any sense, he'd start tagging along on these shopping trips. Because this? This wasn't how things were done back home, where pregnant women were revered like goddesses, not left to wrestle with shopping carts and traffic.

The next day was the start of a sunny weekend, and Aakash proposed, 'Let's go sightseeing today!'

Supriya chimed in, already launching into plans for a fun-filled city tour.

Meanwhile, Debjyoti was stationed in her favourite battlefield, the kitchen. What to make for breakfast? It had to be hearty, filling, and capable of keeping them fuelled for their big day out. And then, like divine intervention, the answer struck her—*luchi* and *aloo dum*! Ah, the puffed, golden clouds of deep-fried joy paired with the rich, spicy potato curry. Her fingers twitched with anticipation.

'How about making some extra *luchis* so we can carry them for lunch?' suggested Supriya.

Debu's heart swelled. 'Absolutely, *beta*! We'll have enough to last us till dinner if need be,' she declared with the confidence of a seasoned matriarch.

With military precision, she set to work. The flour was kneaded, the potatoes boiled, and the mustard oil heated just so—hot enough to make the neighbours wonder. Debjyoti rolled out perfect rounds of *luchi* with the practised ease of a woman who had been feeding her family with both love and mild threats for decades.

The kitchen was alive—oil sizzling, spices sputtering, and the air thick with the tantalising aroma of *hing*, *jeera*, and fried dough. The first batch of *luchis* fluffed up gloriously in the hot oil. Debjyoti beamed. Her cooking was a masterpiece of smells, sounds, and emotions.

And then, disaster struck.

A shrill, piercing wail shattered the idyllic morning. The fire alarm!

Aakash, caught mid-scroll on his phone, yelped and waved a towel over his head like fighting off an invisible swarm of bees. Supriya burst out of her room, flailing her arms wildly, looking ready to abandon ship.

Aakash dashed up the stairs, yelling, 'The fire alarm's gone off!'

Debjyoti, blissfully oblivious, wearing headphones, hummed her favourite Asha Bhosle song as she flipped another *luchi.* Only when Supriya barged into the kitchen, wide-eyed and breathless, did she notice the pandemonium.

'What happened?' Debjyoti asked, confused.

'The fire alarm, Ma! The smoke!' Supriya gestured wildly at the ceiling, where the alarm continued its banshee-like shrieking.

Debjyoti turned off the stove hastily, her hands suddenly unsure. She threw open the windows, and cool air rushed in, carrying away the last wisps of oil-scented smoke. Slowly, the alarm fell silent.

But inside, Debjyoti felt something break.

Her cooking—her love language, her way of holding her children close even across continents—was a hazard in this foreign land. She sank onto a chair, hands trembling.

'What will I do if I can't cook here?' she murmured, eyes glistening. 'Back home, when I fry *begunis*, the neighbours walk in, following the smell. But here? Here, the moment I let mustard oil breathe, the house thinks it's on fire!'

Supriya knelt beside her. 'Oh, Ma. Don't worry. We'll figure it out. Maybe keep a fan running? Or fry things outside?'

Debjyoti shook her head, swallowing the lump in her throat. The fire alarm was telling her that she was in an unfamiliar country and that her way of life was too much.

Aakash put a gentle arm around her. 'Ma, you'll always cook for us. We have to be a little careful. That's all.'

Debjyoti sniffled, then let out a shaky chuckle. 'Fine. But next time, *luchis* will be made in broad daylight with all windows open and fans running at full speed.'

The morning's adventure had taken an unexpected turn, but they would remember it—not just for the food, but for the realisation that no matter where she was, Debjyoti would always be the beating heart of her home, fire alarm be damned. And so the very next day, she decided to cook again.

Debjyoti firmly believed that a pregnant woman's cravings were sacred commandments that must be followed without question. So, this time, she generously turned to Supriya instead of making the menu decision herself.

'What do you feel like eating, *beta*?' she asked.

Supriya stretched out on the sofa. 'Risotto,' she said.

Debjyoti blinked. *Risotto?* What happened to good old *dal-chawal*? Or a nice, hearty paratha with white butter? But no, her daughter had acquired exotic tastes—probably from her husband.

Still, a craving was a craving. With a sigh of great maternal duty, Debjyoti rolled up her sleeves and marched off to battle, ready to conquer the art of making *proper* Italian food… with a bit of help from all those online ladies who cooked and showed. YouTube aunties, Instagram home chefs, and that one suspiciously perfect recipe blog—she had consulted them all.

Meticulously following the recipe she found online for mouthwatering risotto, she began to cook. Debjyoti was a master chef in Bengali cuisine, a decent cook in other Indian dishes, and a total novice in world cuisine. But she loved challenges, and risotto seemed to be one. She had walked to the store the previous day to buy chicken broth, unaware that this Italian dish required a specific type of Italian rice called Arborio rice. 'Well, what can our Basmati not accomplish?' Debjyoti thought as she measured the quantity according to the recipe. But you know what our beloved Basmati cannot achieve? The 'al dente' texture cannot be attained with stirring. Basmati is inherently al dente. Stirring causes the long grains to break and lose their texture. It should be stirred minimally to retain the grain's integrity. However, Debjyoti was unaware of this and thought Basmati was the type of rice used when making a special rice dish, such as pulao or biryani.

The aromas of sautéed onions, garlic, and rice filled the air with the promise of a culinary masterpiece. Her smartphone rested on the countertop, displaying various tabs of risotto recipes, each offering a unique twist on the classic Italian dish. Earphones lodged in her ears played her favourite songs by Lata Mangeshkar.

Debjyoti had a playlist for every occasion. When she wanted to feel youthful, she had Rafi cooing in her ears. When she was driving, she enjoyed Kishore humming for her. When she felt naughty, it was either Geeta Dutt or Asha Bhosle. When she needed to maintain her poise, it was Lata. Today was Lata's day because she needed all the grace and poise in the world. After all, she was cooking risotto.

After checking and cross-referencing multiple recipes, she was confident that this meal would be exceptional. Besides, she needed one without wine, so she decided on one with a touch of lemon and thyme!

As the creamy broth simmered gently, Debjyoti stirred with precision, her wooden spoon gliding effortlessly through the mixture. The fragrance permeating the kitchen grew richer, hinting at the impending gastronomic delight. The recipe instructed stirring, stirring, and stirring some more. With an aching arm,

Debjyoti followed the recipe to the T and stirred. The Basmati rice broke into pieces and disintegrated with the stirring. 'What am I doing?' Debjyoti pondered over her actions. She continued to follow the recipe. 'The risotto smells heavenly but does not look very appetising,' she thought.

Then, she added mushrooms. Mushrooms were something she had never cooked before. She checked online and found that mushrooms should not be washed. 'They need to be showered, not bathed,' the expert had said. 'Do they even know the difference? Have they ever enjoyed a *balti* bath?' She grimaced. She showered the mushrooms, gave them a brush cleanup, and wiped each before adding them to the mixture. Each mushroom was wiped separately.

Once the rice appeared cooked, Debjyoti added a generous dollop of butter and a sprinkling of grated Parmesan, just as the recipe prescribed. She stirred with a flourish, anticipating the creamy texture and indulgent taste of the risotto she had seen in pictures. Achieving an al dente finish was not possible with Basmati rice stirred excessively, so Debjyoti added milk and cooked it a little longer to enhance the dish's creaminess. Well, it did turn out well. After all, the cheese, milk, and butter had to work their magic. What mattered was that the family loved it. Three hours spent researching, preparing, and stirring had been worth it all as Supriya smiled while eating it.

'Doesn't it look familiar?' Debjyoti looked at the risotto and ruminated. It dawned on her that while her hands had been preparing risotto according to the Italian recipe, what she had achieved was something that could have been cooked much more quickly. Before her eyes, she could see a rather pale-looking *khichdi*—a humble Indian comfort food!

The realisation brought a mix of emotions—amusement, confusion, and a strange sense of contentment. She laughed at the irony of her culinary pursuit ending in a dish she could prepare in her sleep. And so, with a wooden spoon in one hand and a heart full of passion in the other, Debjyoti continued to stir, blend, and create dishes for her daughter. This time, she needed no recipe from the Internet. All she had to do was remember the flavours of her childhood and cook with flourish. Call it risotto or call it *khichdi*! What's in a name?

Debjyoti continued to cook every day, noting the colour returning to Supriya's cheeks. Soon, she had to go for a medical checkup, and all should be well.

Sonali

Rajesh narrowed his eyes at the phone screen as he devised a plan for navigating the city. Since arriving in Seattle, he had made it his mission to experience everything: the sculptures, the mountains, the ferries, the museums, and the parks. Meanwhile, Aman was occupied with back-to-back Zoom meetings, and something called a 'code freeze', a technical term that sounded alarming but was routine. Therefore, it fell to Jake—tall, all teeth, and perpetually wearing impossibly white sneakers—to take charge, unwittingly becoming their guide through the unfamiliar city. Not that Sonali minded. Jake was warm and hilarious and somehow got them free samples at every coffee shop they passed.

'Americans are always giving things for free,' Rajesh said, pocketing an oat milk latte.

Aman and Jake's home was… nice. It was a glass-and-steel high-rise downtown. The interiors were all greys and whites—what Sonali privately called the 'corporate aesthetic'. The countertops sparkled perfectly, as though a cleaning service came in every day.

Aman's room was absolutely sterile. A bed, a laptop, a stack of technical books, and—thank heavens—a copy of *Sapiens* made

Sonali feel marginally less anxious about her son becoming a robot in a hoodie. On the other hand, Jake's room was loud and chaotic, with an actual plant named Bert.

Every morning, Rajesh transformed into a brown-skinned Columbus. He'd already tackled Pike Place Market (nearly beheaded by a flying fish), the Space Needle (refused to walk on the glass floor, clutched Sonali's arm like a nervous bride), and the Museum of Pop Culture (stood next to the Nirvana exhibit with the reverence of a man posing beside Rajinikanth's wax statue).

The hike to Rattlesnake Ledge, which is about an hour and a half, had taken exactly 4.5 minutes, after which Rajesh declared that 'views are overrated' and spent the rest of the day recovering on a bench. But he *did* fall in love with clam chowder on the Bainbridge Island ferry.

Today's plan? Chihuly Glass Garden and a sunset cruise. Seattle enveloped them in its drizzle, neon glow, overly polite baristas, and quinoa-forward menus. They had come for Aman, but Jake's Seattle tours had taken precedence.

'We must *maximise* our time,' said Rajesh, brandishing his phone like a weapon of mass scheduling. 'It's not every day we come to *America*!'

Jake, draped on the couch like a lazy housecat, chuckled. 'Dude, you guys are doing more in a week than I've done in six years.'

Rajesh beamed. 'Efficiency, Jake. That's the Indian way.'

Sonali rolled her eyes. She'd seen this man forget his own cousin's wedding anniversary and once wear two different socks to a board meeting—but here, he was Captain Seattle.

Still, she couldn't deny it—something was charming about this version of her husband. His eyes were wide with wonder, questions loaded, always ready with a camera click and an 'ooh' at some sculpture or sunset.

In the apartment, Rajesh was the Alexa monitor. He would look at the sleek black cylinder on the table and enunciate like a theatre actor: 'Alexa, what's the weather tomorrow?'

The calm robotic voice would respond, 'Tomorrow will be sunny, with a high of seventy-five degrees Fahrenheit.'

Rajesh behaved as if Alexa were his personal assistant.

Swaggering out of the room, he would say, 'Alexa, switch on the bedroom.'

Alexa obeyed. Rajesh looked mighty pleased. Right now, he was busy instructing Alexa to play his favourite Engelbert Humperdinck. Alexa was having difficulty understanding his accent. Sonali laughed.

Meanwhile, Aman was in the kitchen, meticulously orchestrating a mini-Indian meal.'Hey Siri,' he said, casually slicing paneer, 'find me a recipe for tikka masala.' Siri obediently rattled off spices and steps, while Aman smoothly added, 'Set a timer for 15 minutes.'

Siri complied like a well-behaved sous-chef.

Sonali was mesmerised by the intelligence surrounding her. Smart thermostats, mood lighting, voice-controlled music, and cook timers that behaved like well-mannered children were all rather excessive.

She watched as gadgets danced around her family. It wasn't as if she didn't *know* about AI. Aman had explained it all, and she had also read up on it. But seeing it all in motion—this seamless, voice-activated ballet of light, sound, and information—was something else.

Back home, her Alexa sulked in the corner until someone remembered that it actually works. Here, they practically had a tech butler.

Still, she smiled. Maybe she didn't need to master it all. Perhaps she could sit back, sip her hot chai (brewed by Aman, timer and all), and let America impress her one gadget at a time.

One evening, as the sun lazily melted into the Seattle skyline, they all sat on the tiny apartment balcony, a cramped little space with exactly two chairs and a questionable folding stool that wobbled if you breathed near it. Sonali had commandeered the comfiest seat, her hands wrapped around a warm cup of chai, while Aman leaned against the railing, scrolling through his phone, only half-listening. Sprawled on the floor with his back against the wall, Jake was doing what he did best—being effortlessly charming.

'So, Aunty, what is it like growing up in India?' he inquired, his blue eyes sparkling with genuine curiosity.

Sonali took a long, appreciative sip of her chai, the steam curling up in the cool evening air. 'Oh, it is... lively. *Full.* Bustling markets where the shopkeepers know your name, where you could haggle for mangoes and talk about their daughter's wedding plans. Festivals where the whole neighbourhood lit up, and everyone's house smelled of ghee and cardamom. Even the fights were communal—if your neighbour had an issue with you, the entire lane would know before you did.'

Jake laughed. 'That sounds kinda like my old neighbourhood.'

Sonali raised an eyebrow. 'Really? I thought you grew up in—what was it? Montana?'

'Idaho,' Jake corrected with a grin. 'Coeur d'Alene. It's a small town with a sense of community. My grandma raised me. She still lives in the same house she's occupied for 50 years. Everyone knows each other's business, and the whole street magically gathers at someone's doorstep when someone bakes a pie. We had a general store where you could find everything from fishing bait to homemade jam.'

Sonali nodded, delighted. 'So you *do* understand.'

Jake shot her finger guns. 'I get it, Aunty.'

Aman snorted and finally looked up from his phone. 'He's been calling you Aunty for two weeks now, Ma. Are you okay with this?'

Sonali waved a hand dismissively. 'He says it with respect. And besides, he listens to my stories, which is more than I can say for *some* people.'

Jake grinned as Aman rolled his eyes.

The conversation flowed effortlessly and warmly, meandering through memories like a gentle river. Sonali reminisced about her childhood Diwali, savouring the thrill of new clothes and the scent of fireworks in the air. Jake shared stories of snowy Christmases, his grandma's famous cinnamon rolls, and the time he fell into a frozen lake while trying to impress a girl in middle school. Despite himself, Aman became engrossed, recounting his memories of summer vacations in India, visiting his grandparents in Kudroli, and Clara Granny, who spoiled him lavishly with sweets and unfiltered opinions.

Almost seamlessly, Alexa was included in the family discourse when Aman instructed, 'Alexa, play Hindi songs from the 1980s.'

Memories revolving around the songs and the movies they were from were recounted, and Aman hummed the tunes along with Alexa, who continued to build the playlist like an all-knowing family member.

Sonali realised that conversations were no longer confined to humans in the modern world. As she went about her daily life, she encountered machines that could respond, mimic, and predict her thoughts. This technological environment, where artificial voices engaged in discussions, fascinated her deeply. At first, Sonali was wary of the GPS in her car. 'We don't know where we are headed, and this gadget knows where we need to go and even suggests the best route to get there,' she often mused.

One evening, while sitting in her dimly lit study, Sonali stared at her computer screen, lost in thought. She had just engaged in an online chat with a customer service bot that, for a moment, felt almost human in its responses. The conversation left her questioning the boundaries between authenticity and artificiality.

Somewhat unsettled, Sonali decided to explore this brave new world further. She initiated conversations with Alexa, who was readily accessible in the living room. She probed her responses with intricate queries that delved into the complexities of human emotions. The answers were remarkably well-crafted and logical. Alexa was polite and quickly apologised for not knowing an answer or for providing an incorrect response. 'I will use my Indian Alexa more when I return,' Sonali decided.

Amid her contemplation, her phone buzzed with a notification. It was a simple message from her closest friend: 'How are you?'

Sonali realised she had been neglecting her genuine connections with fellow humans in her quest to understand the capabilities of machines.

As she responded to her friend's message by calling her, the words flowed effortlessly, reflecting the ease of their years-long companionship. She talked for an hour, free from the pressure of always being correct or apologising for a wrong answer. They laughed at shared memories, the goof-ups they had made, and their lives.

She gushed about Aman and Jake's friendship. 'You won't believe it, *yaar*. They're like Jai and Veeru! A total *jugalbandi*. Jake reminds me of those boys who become *ghar ka bachcha* within minutes. He even calls me Aunty like Indian boys!'

Her friend laughed. '*Bas, bas*, don't get too attached. You'll cry buckets when you have to leave!'

Sonali scoffed but knew it was true. Jake had become an extension of Aman's life and, by default, of hers. She smiled as she sat back, watching Aman and Jake bicker over who would do the dishes. *Jai-Veeru,* indeed.

'Alexa, turn on the living room,' Rajesh's voice filled the room. A short and simple 'Okay' from Alexa, the living room was flooded with bright light.

As the family enjoyed their dinner, their conversations wandered between technology and tradition.

'Okay, so we have a lot of digital convenience, AI caters to every need, but *ek baat hai*,' Sonali pondered, 'any algorithm cannot replace a loving family.'

No soft-spoken digital assistant, no matter how efficient, can ever mimic the warmth of a genuine hug, nor can an emoji quite capture the true laughter of in-person companionship. No algorithm can wipe away the tears that spring from the depths of human emotion. Human connection, composed of whispered secrets and unspoken understanding, rises beyond the sterile precision of machines.

And then, as darkness fell and the family moved towards their rooms, Rajesh took command, bidding, 'Alexa, shut the living room,' much like performing a magic act. Alexa, like a genie, enveloped the room in darkness. As Sonali nestled into her sheets, she too indulged in tech banter, chiming, 'Alexa, wake me up at 6.00 a.m., please.' With all the calm and assurance of a sage, the AI responded, 'Okay,' leaving the night sprinkled with a hint of whimsy.

This sabbatical had tossed Sonali miles away from her carefully structured life back in India. As a dedicated professor and a prominent figure in academic circles, she had embarked on this temporary escape with excitement and trepidation. True, she was technically on a break from teaching, but what about her research? Ha! That beast never slept. She had made all sorts of noble promises—'*Haan, haan*, I'll attend research meetings from here, no problem!'—and now, thanks to the miserable twelve-hour time difference, her days were American, and her nights were Indian.

Young faculty always required her to supervise dissertations, attend Research Degree Committee meetings, and present at seminars. Sabbatical? This was turning out to be a full-time job in a different time zone.

Every night before a meeting, the clock on the wall taunted her. It ticked forward at a snail's pace. Simultaneously, she stared at it with sleep-deprived eyes, awaiting the inevitable moment when her laptop screen would light up and someone from her university would pop in with a 'Good morning, ma'am!' At the same time, she sat there at midnight clutching a mug of chai like a life raft.

One such peaceful night, her mind wandered as she drummed her fingers against the desk, waiting for a particularly high-maintenance research scholar to join. She thought of Aman and how he had battled this situation every time he visited India. '*Arrey*, poor thing! No wonder he used to pass out at odd hours on the sofa like a drugged puppy!'

The realisation hit hard. Every time she complained about his nocturnal work schedules, rolled her eyes at their odd mealtimes, or snapped at Aman for dozing off during family lunches, she didn't understand. But now—*uff!*—she got it—the sheer, bone-deep exhaustion of battling against a clock that wasn't hers.

Her thoughts drifted back to her student days—the endless research papers, and the thrill of an unexpected breakthrough at 2.00 a.m. She had always taken pride in her discipline, work ethic, and commitment to never missing a research meeting. But today, sitting in a dimly lit room halfway across the world, she felt something different, a kind of solidarity.

During the meeting, as her colleague's voice cracked over a poor-quality microphone and another's child wailed in the background, Sonali smiled. *Sab ek jaise hi hain*! (Everyone is the same!) Whether in Delhi or Seattle, whether newcomers or seasoned academics, they were all simply weary souls grappling with bandwidth issues and time zones, clinging to their love of research.

She stretched, yawning, and grinned to herself. 'The sun never stops shining, right?'

And just as she switched off the lights and shuffled off to her bedroom, she saw Jake.

Padding across the living room, barefoot and entirely at ease, he walked straight into Aman's room.

Sonali blinked.

'*Arrey?*'

What was he doing up at *2:30 a.m.*? Had he forgotten his charger? Was he borrowing a book? Maybe they had a last-minute work thing—'Tech-*wale toh hamesha aise hi rehte hain, na?* (Tech people are always like this, right?) Always on their laptops, typing furiously, working at ungodly hours….'

She waited.

She wasn't *snooping*, okay? She was just… curious. Just making sure everything was fine.

One minute passed. Then two. Then five.

Jake didn't come out.

Sonali felt a small, odd knot tighten in her stomach. '*Bus yaar*,' she told herself. 'It's nothing. Go to sleep.'

But as she went to her room, her mind wouldn't quiet down. The image of Jake disappearing into Aman's room played on a loop. Had he dozed off in there? Were they having some deep, brooding conversation?

It was none of her business. Absolutely none.

And yet, sleep didn't come easily that night.

Radhika

The automatic doors sighed open, and Radhika appeared, tall and unhurried, as if she were strolling in her Haryana fields rather than at Seattle-Tacoma International Airport. Her navy-blue salwar kameez was crisp, despite the flight, and the dupatta was draped around her shoulders, while her long, dark hair flowed down her back in a thick braid that no turbulence dared to disturb.

Vikram spotted her instantly. She looked the same—regal, collected, and utterly confident in a place where most travellers looked like lost luggage.

'Ma,' he said, stepping forward, laptop bag still slung across his shoulder, his tie slightly loosened. 'What… a sudden surprise!'

She smiled as if they'd planned this for weeks. '*Tu nahi aa saka, toh socha main hi aa jaaun.* (You can't come, so I thought I should come.) Simple.'

He blinked. 'You flew across the world without planning the trip with me?'

'You're busy,' she said with a shrug, as if it were an accepted family trait, like being left-handed or disliking *karela*. 'And now look—I'm here.'

In the car, while Vikram silently calculated how to rearrange a week packed with reviews and client calls, she pulled out a tiffin box. '*Methi ke paranthe.* The real welcome package.'

'Ma, this is a company car—'

'*Bas, bas.* Don't start with your rules. *Main thodi na kha rahi hoon, tu khayega.* (I'm not the one eating, you're going to eat.)'

As the Seattle cityscape passed by, Vikram exhaled slowly. His mother had landed unplanned, and she never does anything without a plan.

Early next morning, Radhika was in Vikram's kitchen at 6.42 a.m., examining a fridge that, in her opinion, belonged to a man either on a diet or in distress.

'One bottle of almond milk, two sad tomatoes, and hummus?' she muttered. '*Yeh toh shraadh ka thaal lag raha.* (This looks like a *shraadh* plate.)'

She had already swept the living room with her eyes the night before—white walls, expensive-looking but cold. A man who lived here paid his taxes on time but forgot to soak rice.

In her rose-pink cotton salwar kameez, hair in a neat plait, she looked like she had been here since forever and not just landed from across the world. Her hands moved with the speed of muscle memory—washing, chopping, tempering. By the time Vikram shuffled into the kitchen, hair still wet from a rushed shower, the apartment smelled like home.

'Ma, it's too early. And what is that smell?'

'Ghee. From *your* suitcase. I packed a steel dabba.'

'You carried ghee in an international check-in?'

'Of course. I trust it more than your oat milk.'

He sighed and poured himself a coffee. She handed him a plate of *poha* garnished with fresh coriander. 'Eat while it's hot. And stop drinking black water.'

He took a bite. Warm. Comforting. Familiar.

'Ma, you don't have to do all this.'

She looked up from wiping the counter. '*Beta*, I didn't come to see Seattle. I came to *see* you.'

That's what she did. She ensured that Vikram was well-fed, the house was well-maintained, and the garden was well-tended.

One morning, amid the household's hustle and bustle, a sudden quiet fell. All the electrical appliances stopped humming. 'It's a power outage!' Vikram exclaimed, rushing out of his room to check the electricity mains in the garage. Working from home, he needed to be available on his laptop round the clock. Radhika realised that it meant trouble for her. The electric stove was off as well, and the mutton was left waiting to be cooked. 'The furnace won't work either,' Vikram informed, frustration clear in his voice.

As they considered the situation, Radhika, thinking about the upcoming inconveniences, reflected on the stark contrast between India and the US. In India, power outages were frequent, and people depended on inverters and generators. But in the US, such outages were so rare that people counted them on their fingertips and discussed them in the news. Radhika could herself recall a few.

'The power will be back in two hours,' Vikram announced, reading intently from his mobile. He had an important meeting and needed to be constantly connected, and his worry was writ large on his face.

With the phones on the verge of dying, laptops going to sleep, the television rendered useless, and the Internet down, Radhika knew they would have to make do without modern conveniences. 'Cold lunch it is,' she mused, hoping the power would be restored soon. While Vikram continued to update her on the estimated time of power restoration, Radhika accepted the situation. She stepped out into the garden, seeking solace in the greenery. The sun above shone brightly, illuminating the foliage around her. An avid gardener, Radhika decided to begin with weeding. Squatting in her wide-brimmed straw hat, she picked weeds from the flower beds and noticed her neighbours emerging from their houses. People started chatting with one another, discussing the unexpected outage. Some took their dogs for a walk and waved a cheery hello to Radhika as they passed her house.

Families came into their yards, stood around talking, and enjoyed a moment of unexpected freedom. It felt like a throwback to simpler times when people relied on each other for entertainment and camaraderie. 'Like back home in my farmlands,' thought Radhika. This is what man is supposed to do. Grow food, flowers, plants, and crops and take the blessings of Mother Earth.

As the hours passed, Radhika unexpectedly did the happy dance instead of having a meltdown. The universe had slyly hit the pause button on their hyper-connected lives, and Radhika was there for it. Even Vikram had joined her briefly in the garden, telling her that his plants were indigenous to promote sustainability. Radhika, the expert farmer, listened with bemused indulgence. This outage had flipped the script on the wired world, forcing people to have real conversations and reminding them that there's a thing called 'fresh air' outside their pixelated caves.

So, as they crawled back into their virtual cocoons that night, Radhika lay there with a satisfied grin. It had been a happy day for her. Despite the blackout, they had stumbled upon a path of togetherness. It was like finding a Wi-Fi hotspot for the soul—something not even the most high-tech gadget could conjure.

That night, amidst the silent hum of charging cables, Radhika reflected. With a heart full of quirky hope, she planned, 'I am going to create such moments for Vikram and me. I will grow real vegetables in his backyard and feed him fresh produce. I have to prepare him before we have our talk.'

Vikram casually mentioned a weekend trek the next morning, and Radhika jumped at the opportunity.

'*Beta, tu ja raha hai toh main bhi chaloon?* (Son, if you're going, can I come too?)' she said, packing some *besan laddus* into a steel dabba.

Vikram gave her a sceptical look. 'Maa, it's a trek. Not a picnic.'

'So? We deal with land and farms all the time back home. Your father used to run through the fields all day. I'm used to this!'

And that was that.

As they drove towards the Rainier, Radhika sat in the passenger seat, peering out at the thick forests, winding roads, and the distant snow-capped peak.

'It's nice,' she muttered, nodding.

Vikram smirked. 'Wow, high praise, Ma. Just "nice"?'

She sniffed. 'Well, it's good, but nothing compared to the Himalayas.'

Vikram groaned. 'Ma, why do you always do this?'

'I'm just stating facts! The Himalayas are the Himalayas—sacred, powerful, and home to Lord Shiva himself! Have you ever seen Mansarovar? That's a truly remarkable mountain experience, combining spirituality and grandeur. This one here… it's just sitting there with a white blanket on top.' She gestured at the distant peak dismissively.

Vikram rolled his eyes. 'Right. Because American mountains don't have "*power*".'

'Power is everywhere, but you only *feel* it when you hear temple bells ringing, see saints meditating, or stop at a tiny tea stall where half the mountain's trekkers are sipping hot chai.'

Vikram grinned. 'Ma, you just want a tea stall at 14,000 feet, don't you?'

She sighed dramatically. 'If they set up a proper tea stall here, then maybe I'd consider calling this a real mountain.'

By the time they reached the base camp, Vikram was laughing, and Radhika was still grumbling about how Americans made too much fuss over one mountain.

The trek started, and Radhika, full of confidence, strode along. The air was crisp, the views spectacular, and she kept up just OK for the first few kilometres.

Then, the incline got steeper.

And her *mountain spirit* began to feel a little less enthusiastic.

She stopped to catch her breath. 'Hmm… this is… quite… steep….'

Vikram smirked. 'Yeah, Ma. Welcome to trekking.'

'Shut up. Your mother has walked the path to Kedarnath on foot. I need… a small break.'

She waved him ahead, pretending to admire the view while

secretly massaging her knees. Vikram, assuming she'd turn back, trekked on.

But Radhika was *chhoron se aage* (ahead of boys), remember? Giving up wasn't in her blood.

She continued alone, determined to prove a point—to whom, even she wasn't sure. The trees thinned, the rocks became sharper, and she walked slowly but steadily. Somewhere along the way, she forgot about proving anything. The mountain was silent, save for the crunch of her footsteps and the occasional birdcall. The crisp air filled her lungs, and she felt truly at peace for the first time since arriving in America.

When Vikram returned to the trailhead and found her missing, panic set in.

'Where's my mom?' he asked a group of trekkers resting nearby.

One of them shrugged. 'Last I saw, she was still climbing.'

Vikram's stomach dropped. 'Climbing?! Alone?'

He turned and sprinted back up the trail, muttering curses under his breath.

Meanwhile, Radhika, oblivious to the commotion below, reached a clearing. The mountain lay before her in all its expansive, snow-covered splendour, with clouds drifting lazily around the peak.

She exhaled. 'Okay, fine. It's nice.'

Then she heard Vikram's voice echoing through the mountains. 'Maaa!!'

She turned to see him bounding up the trail, his face a mix of relief and fury.

'Why are you shouting?' she asked, hands on her hips.

'Ma! You scared the hell out of me! I thought you got lost!'

She scoffed. 'Lost? I'm Radhika. If I don't lose my way in the fields of Haryana, why would I get lost here?'

Vikram doubled over, catching his breath. 'You *cannot* just wander off like this.'

'Oh, please! I was enjoying the view. After all the effort I put into getting here, why rush back?'

Vikram shook his head, but he couldn't help smiling. 'Fine, fine. Did the mountain impress you at least?'

Radhika looked around one last time. The silence, the snow, the way the peak stood tall like an ancient guardian—it wasn't the Himalayas. But it had something.

She patted Vikram's cheek. 'Alright, I admit. It's *a little* nice.'

Vikram groaned. '*A little?*'

Radhika winked. 'If they set up a chai stall here, it might be truly impressive.'

Mother and son laughed together and walked towards the car.

As Vikram manoeuvred the car down the winding roads from Mount Rainier, Radhika sat in the passenger seat, watching the towering trees blur past. The cool mountain air still clung to her skin, but her mind was elsewhere. She had been waiting for the right moment to bring up the topic, and with the breathtaking mountains behind them, it felt like now or never.

She cleared her throat. 'Vikram *beta*, I was thinking….'

Vikram, still riding the high of their trek, glanced at her. 'Hmm?'

'You should come back to India.'

The car didn't swerve, but Vikram's hands tightened on the wheel. He exhaled, already anticipating the conversation. 'Ma….'

'Listen to me,' she said, cutting him off before he could protest. 'I know you love it here. Big offices, big salaries, fancy technology. But what about your land? Your people? The work I've done?'

'Ma, I know you've expanded the business. And I'm proud of you. But—'

'But what?' She turned slightly, facing him. '*Beta*, land is everything. It's permanent. Generations before us worked the same soil we do today. It's ours—no one can take it from us. Here? You're building someone else's dreams, making someone else richer.'

Vikram sighed. 'Ma, it's not like that. The work I do here is meaningful. It's about sustainability, efficiency—'

'And that's exactly why I need you back,' Radhika said firmly. 'Do you realise how much the world is changing? Agriculture is more than just ploughing fields. Farming encompasses the use of AI, automation, and smart irrigation. Even the government is advocating for new-age farming. I've already implemented drip irrigation on some of our lands and installed solar panels to power the water pumps. But I need someone who thoroughly understands this modern technology. I need you.'

Vikram was silent for a moment. She had never spoken about this so directly before. He had seen her resilience and her business acumen, but he had always assumed she was managing everything well. Now, she was saying she needed him.

'Ma, you're already doing great things,' he said carefully. 'But my work here—'

'You can do the same work back home. Build something that belongs to *us.* Imagine bringing the innovation they have here to our business. Smart greenhouses, precision farming, climate-resistant crops… *our* land can lead the way. Why should we wait for foreign companies to come and tell us how to manage our farms?'

Vikram ran a hand through his hair. 'It's not that simple, Ma.'

'It is *beta.* You have the skill. We have the land. Combine them, and we don't just survive—we thrive. Do you think big tech is the future? Let me tell you, farming is the future. The world will always need food. And food comes from the land, not from these big glass buildings or some server room.'

Vikram let out a small laugh. 'Ma, you make it sound like I work in a dark basement.'

She smiled but kept going. 'I know it's a big decision. I won't press you. I hoped you could think about it. We have something genuine back home—something enduring. Can you say the same about this place?'

Vikram didn't answer right away. He focused on the road ahead, but Radhika could tell her words had landed. The conversation wasn't over. She was a farmer. She knew when the seed had been planted. Now, she just had to wait and see if it would take root.

Mona

Neetu's apartment was a compact, one-bedroom rental in a quiet, tree-lined neighbourhood near the University of Washington. It had just enough space to be functional but lacked the frills Mona would have insisted on. The walls were a crisp white, the floors were worn but polished hardwood, and the large, uncurtained windows let in generous slices of Seattle's moody, shifting light.

The furniture was just like a college student's pre-loved collection. A thrifted wooden dining table that doubled as a study desk, a well-loved couch adorned with a chunky knit throw, and a minimalist bedframe pushed against the far wall, draped in soft, earthy-toned sheets. Books were stacked in uneven piles on every available surface, alongside a few small potted plants adding colour to the room. A single framed print of an architectural sketch hung above the desk, its muted lines constituting the only piece of art in the apartment—unless you counted the post-its stuck to the fridge, reminding Neetu to buy oat milk and send emails.

The kitchen was tiny but efficient—open shelves lined with mismatched ceramic mugs, glass jars filled with grains and spices, and precisely two wine glasses because Neetu rarely had time for entertaining. The place smelled faintly of brewed coffee and something fresh—maybe eucalyptus or sage—lingering from a candle she'd burned the night before.

Mona took it all when she stepped through the door, her sharp, kohl-lined eyes scanning the space with the precision of a home appraiser. 'No curtains?' she remarked, toeing off her heels and stepping onto the hardwood floor.

Neetu shrugged, tossing her keys onto the table. 'I like the light. Besides, the house comes with blinds.'

Mona hummed in response, trailing her fingers over the simple wooden desk. 'And no TV?'

'I don't need one.'

Mona sighed dramatically as she sank onto the couch. 'Neetu, this is not a home. This is—' she gestured vaguely around her, '—a setup.'

Neetu grinned, unbothered. 'Exactly. My setup!' she said with a smile. 'I have, however, ordered something to serve as your wardrobe.'

Neetu pointed toward a flat-packed monster in the centre of the living room. The website had promised a DIY cabinet that would be stylish, sleek, and oh-so-modern. But they hadn't mentioned that it would arrive with an instruction manual written by a sadist.

'Alright, let's do this!' she announced to no one in particular, cracking her knuckles. 'Do you want to freshen up, Mom, while I figure this out?' asked Neetu.

From the couch, Mona raised a regal eyebrow. '*Beta*, I don't understand why you didn't just buy a ready-made one. I give you enough allowance. Why suffer?'

'Because it's empowering, Mom! And same-day delivery was only available for DIY kits.'

Mona sighed dramatically as she picked up her purse and headed towards the bedroom. 'Yes, yes. "Empowering." That's what they said about childbirth, too. But I remember the pain.'

Undeterred, Neetu plonked herself on the floor and began unpacking. Wooden panels, screws, bolts, a tiny wrench, and an Allen key she'd probably lose in ten minutes. With its mysterious diagrams of gender-neutral stick figures, the manual sat on top like a challenge.

'Okay, Step 1. Identify all parts. Should be simple, right?'

Forty-five minutes later, Neetu had created what resembled an archaeological dig site, complete with tiny screws and panels. Mona had changed into her pyjamas and observed from her perch, sipping chai. '*Beta*, I think that's a leg you've put as the top.'

'WHAT?!' Neetu scrambled to check, knocking over a pile of screws in the process. 'No, no, it's fine. It's just… an abstract approach.'

Mona tutted. 'Your father once tried to fix a leaky pipe. We had to call a plumber to fix his fixing.'

'Ma, please, this is different. This is interior decor.'

An hour in, Neetu was in a heated battle with two particularly stubborn panels that refused to align. She gritted her teeth. 'Oh, so you want to fight. Fine, let's fight.'

Mona clicked her tongue. '*Beta*, this is why God made carpenters.'

'And why did God make YouTube?' Neetu shot back, grabbing her phone and furiously searching for 'How to assemble a DIY cabinet without losing your mind'.

Two hours, three coffee refills, and one minor existential crisis later, Neetu stood back, triumphant. 'LOOK AT THIS BEAUTY!' she declared, admiring the now-assembled cabinet standing proudly in the corner.

Mona, who had been silently recording the entire ordeal, grinned. 'Oh, I have looked. And I have proof.'

Neetu narrowed her eyes. 'What did you do?'

Mona smirked, turning the phone around to reveal an expertly edited eight-minute video montage—clips of Neetu struggling, swearing, and talking to inanimate objects, all set to an upbeat Bollywood track.

Neetu gasped. 'Ma! You posted this?!'

'Of course! You're viral, *beta*. There are already fifty comments! People love a woman who DIYs and doesn't quit. Also, one aunty has asked if you do modular kitchens.'

Neetu groaned, but she couldn't help grinning. 'Well, at least I won the battle. And this cabinet is officially Mom-approved.'

Mona patted the cabinet. 'Yes, yes. Very sturdy. Just don't keep anything breakable on top.'

Mother and daughter laughed and plonked on the recliner, ready to watch a newly released Hindi movie.

The next morning, Mona woke early, perhaps due to jet lag, while Neetu was already awake, as that had become her habit. Neetu handed Mona a hot cup of tea as she sat on the high stool in the kitchen. Mona looked at Neetu with motherly affection. She saw a striking young woman with effortless, natural charm. Neetu had thick, wavy black hair tied in a messy bun when she was deeply engrossed in her work. Her sharp, expressive eyes—dark and inquisitive—constantly scanned her surroundings, taking in details with quiet intensity. Her skin bore a warm, sun-kissed glow from her outdoor projects and hands-on architectural work.

Neetu adjusted the strap of her canvas tote bag as she sipped her oat milk latte, eyeing her mother, who was still staring at her.

'Mom, I was thinking we could go to the Chihuly Garden and Glass today,' Neetu said, her voice hopeful. 'You'd love it—the colours, the details, the way the light plays through the glass. It's like nothing you've seen before.'

Mona didn't even look up. 'Hmm? That sounds nice, *beta*, but I thought we could drive to Portland instead. Tax-free shopping, Neetu! Dior, Gucci, Prada—no sales tax!' She finally glanced up, eyes gleaming with excitement. 'Imagine the deals!'

Neetu sighed. 'You flew from India to see me, and the first thing you want to do is buy handbags?'

Mona's perfectly shaped eyebrows arched. 'I can do both, darling. I have mastered the art of multitasking.' She grinned, slipping her phone into her Birkin bag. 'And I haven't been to Portland in years. It'll be a fun road trip. We can spend some quality time together.'

'Quality time?' Neetu crossed her arms. 'Ma, you'll be inside boutiques all day, and I'll just be standing there while you debate between two shades of beige.'

Mona waved a dismissive hand. 'Neetu, you're young, but one day you'll understand the thrill of a good handbag. It's not just an accessory—it's an investment.'

Neetu gave her a look. 'Mom, it's a purse, not real estate.'

Mona scoffed. 'Spoken like someone who has never owned a Chanel.'

Neetu groaned. 'Fine. But can we at least go to Chihuly first?'

Mona tapped her manicured fingers on the table, feigning thought. 'How about I treat you to lunch at that organic, locally sourced, plant-based spot you adore, and we head to Portland in exchange?'

Neetu narrowed her eyes. 'Mom—'

Mona winked. 'That's my final offer.'

Neetu exhaled sharply, shaking her head. 'You are impossible.'

Mona smiled victoriously. 'And yet, you love me.'

Neetu rolled her eyes, but couldn't help but nod to the plans made by her excited mother.

They loaded into Neetu's car, a used Subaru Outback, a favourite among Seattle's college students and young professionals. Practical, reliable, and designed for the city's rainy weather, it effortlessly blended into the Pacific Northwest. The deep green paint bore a few scratches from parallel parking mishaps, and the interior carried the faint scent of old coffee, which Neetu did not drink but kept in a pouch in a hidden corner of the car.

The backseat was a mix of textbooks, a reusable water bottle, and a couple of reusable grocery bags. A small sticker on the rear windshield read '*Keep Earth Wild*'. The trunk usually held her hiking boots and a rolled-up yoga mat, just in case. Mona plonked her large Birkin on the back seat next to Neetu's canvas tote bag. 'I've got to get her a new car,' she thought.

As Neetu drove towards Portland, Mona glanced at Neetu, taking in her daughter's effortless, almost indifferent style. She always wore loose linen shirts, well-worn jeans, and those same sturdy sneakers—practical, comfortable, utterly devoid of flair. Not a hint of jewellery except for that single silver ring Mona herself had given her years ago, a rare sentimental touch in her otherwise no-nonsense wardrobe.

Mona sighed inwardly. Neetu had always been like this—minimalist, unfazed by luxury, favouring earthy tones over anything remotely glamorous. And yet, something was striking about her. With her tall, slender frame and that quiet, confident stride, she moved like someone who knew exactly where she was going—'Even if she hadn't figured out every step yet, or perhaps she had, and I don't know about it,' she shrugged.

Once in Portland, Mona did not waste a second and entered the Chanel store to pick up the structured leather handbag on display. Neetu stared at the price tag, her eyebrows shooting up so high they practically disappeared into her hairline.

'Mom, this is ridiculous,' she hissed, holding up the handbag, the colour of burnt caramel. 'Two thousand dollars? For a *bag*?'

Mona, unfazed, examined a sleek black tote, running her manicured fingers over the buttery soft leather. 'A *classic*.' She turned to the sales associate, flashing her most charming smile. 'Do you have this in navy?'

Neetu exhaled sharply, crossing her arms.

Mona barely glanced at her. 'Oh, my poor, practical child. You'll understand one day.'

But Neetu *wouldn't* understand. Not now, not ever.

To her, this was frivolity at its height—an utterly unnecessary splurge on something that, in her view, served the same purpose as a cotton tote bag from the university bookstore. But for Mona, it was about control. It was about filling the hollow spaces in her life, the ones Sandeep had carved out with his lies and betrayals. Mona couldn't fix her marriage. She couldn't undo the years of deception. But she *could* walk out of this boutique with a Chanel.

And yet, here was Neetu, standing in front of her with that disapproving frown, her sturdy sneakers tapping against the floor, looking at her mother like she was a lost cause.

Mona sighed and placed the black tote back on the display. 'Fine. No bag.'

Neetu looked relieved. 'Great. Now, can we please go to eat?'

Mona exhaled, glancing at the sparkling designer displays around her one last time. 'Fine,' she said, linking arms with her daughter. Of course, they couldn't do Portland and Chihuly in one day, so they settled for lunch at Neetu's favourite café and talked about her life at the university. Chihuly will have to wait for a week. They wandered around the Saturday Market, admiring all the handmade artefacts, shared a doughnut from the famous outlet, and spent a lazy but lovely day.

Seattle was proving to be full of surprises. Mona had anticipated moody weather, overzealous baristas, and an abundance of techies in fleece jackets—but she hadn't expected how much she would enjoy exploring the city alone. She had no alternative, as Neetu was at the university all week.

Mona had found a game room with an absurdly polished pool table, a swimming pool with a jacuzzi that gurgled invitingly, and—her personal favourite—a dog park bursting with tail-wagging energy. Every evening, she'd perch on a bench and watch Seattle's elite canines frolic about, tails wagging, paws skidding, their owners cooing in various tones of indulgence. It reminded her of Cheeku and Sundae, her two fur babies, whom she had left behind in India, and for a moment, the city's grey skies didn't seem so gloomy.

Then, one day, something bizarre happened.

At the park, a woman in neon workout gear suddenly cranked up a portable speaker and launched into a full-blown dance session—hip thrusts, arm waves, the works. Before Mona could process what was happening, her feet had betrayed her, dragging her straight into the middle of the madness. The beats were catchy. The crowd was laughing, and Mona—fashionable, poised, *dignified* Mona—was flinging her arms around like she was at a Punjabi wedding after two Patiala pegs.

It became a thing. Every evening, she showed up, twirled around with the ladies, and went home feeling slightly ridiculous but weirdly happy.

Then, one night, over dinner, Neetu, her ever-practical, no-nonsense daughter, dropped the bomb.

'Mom, you know that's a fitness class, right?'

Mona stopped mid-bite. 'What?'

'Yeah, that lady in pink? She's the instructor. People *pay* to be in that class.'

Mona's stomach did an unpleasant flip. Good lord. She had been joyfully gate-crashing a workout session, shaking her tail feathers while everyone else was burning calories. How embarrassing.

The following evening, she attempted to sneak past the park unnoticed, but just as she was about to make a clean escape, someone shouted, 'Mona! Where are you going?'

She turned, flushed and flustered. 'I-I just realised I might have… um, intruded. I didn't know it was a class. I'm so sorry, I'll—'

'Oh, please,' a woman with bouncy curls said, rolling her eyes. 'We *love* having you here.'

Another one grinned conspiratorially. 'Besides, we all know who you are. You're Nitya's mom!'

And just like that, Seattle had given her a new identity—Nitya's mum. And you know what? Mona realised she loved it.

Mona felt a strange warmth seep into her. Despite her no-nonsense, slightly detached demeanour, Neetu wasn't just some lonely nerd buried in blueprints and sustainability projects. People liked her. They respected her, even. Mona had overheard it often—at the café where they had grabbed a coffee, where a barista greeted Neetu with easy familiarity, and outside the university, where a classmate had called out, 'Hey, Nitz! See you at the panel tomorrow?' with the kind of casual admiration Mona was familiar with.

She smiled, watching Neetu absentmindedly tuck her hair into a bun while unpacking groceries. She might dress like a monk, but clearly, she had her own little tribe.

Talking of tribes. Mona already regretted saying yes to this dinner. Meeting Neetu's boyfriend? In a fancy Seattle restaurant with mood lighting and waiters who probably had PhDs in gastronomy. She'd rather be in Portland, drowning her loneliness in tax-free Gucci.

But here she was.

'This is Ayaan,' Neetu said, as casually as if she were introducing a lab partner, not the man she was supposedly seeing. 'Ayaan, my mom.'

Mona looked up and—oh ho. Tall. Broad shoulders. Crisp white shirt, sleeves neatly folded to reveal a Cartier on his wrist. The kind of expensive-looking stubble that suggested he spent more on beard grooming than most people did on skincare.

And those dimples. Sheesh.

'Hello, Aunty,' he said smoothly, leaning in just the right amount, not too stiff or casual. 'I've heard so much about you.'

Mona arched an eyebrow. 'Have you?'

Ayaan grinned, utterly unruffled. 'Nitya talks about you all the time.'

Hmph. Smooth talker. She'd met his type before.

Meanwhile, Neetu was scanning the menu, looking for something all three could agree upon.

Mona watched Ayaan reach for the wine list. His fingers—long, graceful—flipped through the pages as if he had been doing this all his life. 'Shall we get the Château Margaux?' he suggested, glancing at Neetu, then Mona. 'It pairs well with—'

'I don't drink, remember?' Neetu interrupted, her tone flat.

'Of course. But I am sure Aunty will have something,' Ayaan smiled, turning towards Mona. 'Maybe something lighter? A Pinot, perhaps?'

Mona bit back a snort. This boy. He wasn't just rich—he was old-money rich—the kind that didn't blink at four-figure dinner tabs or spontaneous weekend getaways.

'So,' she asked, swirling her water like a martini. 'What do you do, Ayaan?'

He leaned back, easy, confident. 'I handle acquisitions for my family's company. We're mostly in luxury hospitality.'

Ah. Of course.

'Last month, I was in Bora Bora, finalising a deal,' he added. 'Incredible place. The water is unreal—crystal clear. You must visit sometime, Aunty.'

Mona could feel Neetu stiffen beside her. However, she looked towards Ayaan and said, 'Right now, she is here, Ayaan, for a vacation.'

Mona pressed her lips together, watching the two of them. The way Ayaan's fingers brushed Neetu's hand absentmindedly, the way Neetu let him.

Mona sat back, fingers tightening around the stem of her water glass, her practised smile in place but her mind whirring. Ayaan was everything she had feared—polished, privileged, and far too charming for his own good. She knew his type, having spent years watching men like him manoeuvre through life with their effortless smiles and bottomless bank accounts, never quite needing to try. And Neetu, her idealistic, fiercely independent daughter—what was she doing with someone like this? Mona had imagined Neetu with a fellow nerd, a socially awkward climate activist, or maybe an overenthusiastic architect who sketched floor plans in his sleep. Not… this. Not a smooth-talking heir to a luxury empire who probably flew private and never worried about the price of organic groceries. The thought sat heavy in her stomach, along with the gnawing fear that Neetu, so firm in her principles, might be slipping into a world Mona had long stopped believing in—the world of trust and love and happily-ever-afters.

CHAPTER 4

The Rewrite Circle

The Hindu Temple shimmered under the golden glow of hundreds of diyas and fairy lights strung across its arched entrance. The air was thick with the mingling aromas of incense, fresh flowers, and the rich, buttery scent of *prasad* distributed in small leaf bowls. Inside, the deities stood adorned in silk and jewels, with little Krishna in a silver cradle at the centre of the altar, ready for the midnight birth celebration. Devotees moved in rhythmic waves—some stood in quiet prayer, while others sang bhajans, their voices rising and falling with the beats of the *dholak*.

It felt like a night dipped in magic, glitter, and a lot of ghee. One could almost imagine Krishna himself—mischief in his eyes and butter on his lips—pulling the invisible strings to gather every Indian within a five-mile radius of the temple. Of course, only he could throw a birthday party where people arrive in silks, fast all day, and still smile for selfies next to baby idols in cradles.

Krishna's birth marked the arrival of hope amid chaos. True to character, this Indian God flirted, philosophised, stole butter, and dropped a Gita-sized truth bomb, teaching us to act according to circumstance.

In his world, work wasn't separate from play, mischief wasn't separate from meaning, and even detachment was tinged with storytelling. He was a divine figure who reminded us that life could be both messy and magnificent.

Pulled by this invisible string, our heroines arrived at the temple with their families, wearing the finest desi attires they had brought from India.

Sugandha clutched her *pallu* as she stepped inside, eyes scanning the familiar yet foreign surroundings. The chants of 'Hare Krishna' felt like home, but the sea of unfamiliar faces—Indians of all accents and backgrounds—reminded her that she was far from Andhra. A small child dressed as Krishna ran past her, his golden *mukut* slipping sideways. She smiled, momentarily transported back to the days when she would dress Sharath in a tiny yellow dhoti for Janmashtami celebrations at home.

Across the temple courtyard, Radhika, dressed in an elegant green cotton salwar kameez, watched the temple volunteers efficiently organise the *prasad* distribution. She was impressed—everything was so orderly, yet there was still that vibrant chaos of an Indian festival. When she spotted a large brass vessel of *makhan-mishri prasad*, she chuckled, thinking of how Vikram refused to eat it as a child.

Ever the observer, Sonali took in the details—the elaborate rangoli at the entrance, the intricate torans hanging from the pillars, the priest chanting *shlokas* fluently in Sanskrit. At the same time, an American-born teenager beside him tried to follow along. She noted how effortlessly cultures blended here—the temple-goers wore everything from traditional salwar suits to jeans and jackets, and the bhajan singers included elderly ladies in saris and young men in hoodies.

Mona adjusted the dupatta over her shoulder, scanning the crowd. She wasn't deeply religious, but she did enjoy the spectacle of it all. She had been to grander temples in India and Malaysia, but something about how NRIs held onto their traditions here fascinated her. A group of women stood together at the side, passing around a tray of homemade sweets, their laughter ringing through the temple hall.

Debjyoti, standing slightly apart, was absorbed in the kirtan. Supriya nudged her playfully. 'Ma, you look so serious! It's just like back home, isn't it?'

Debjyoti smiled. 'Yes... and no. The spirit is the same, but look at them,' she gestured to a group of children reciting Sanskrit verses. 'They are learning these *shlokas* in a foreign land. It makes me proud.'

As the clock struck twelve noon, anticipation filled the atmosphere. 'Traditionally, the ceremony would be conducted at midnight in India,' thought Sonali, watching from a distance, 'but considering the work schedules and time limitations of Indians here, all festivals were accommodated. Even our gods are tolerant like that!' she smiled to herself. The crowd pushed forward to witness the ritual of rocking little Krishna's cradle. The priest's voice resounded: '*Nand ke anand bhayo, Jai Kanhaiya Lal ki!*' The hall burst into a joyous chorus, bells ringing, conches blowing, and hands clapping in harmony.

At that moment, the five women stood together amidst the chants and celebrations. They exchanged glances—some amused, some thoughtful, others lost in reflection. In a temple thousands of miles from home, they had unknowingly drawn towards one another, united by a shared culture, nostalgia, and an unspoken understanding.

And perhaps, unknowingly, this was the beginning of something new.

As the final aarti concluded and the 'Govinda Gopala' echoes faded, the devotees slowly moved towards the langar hall, where the Janmashtami feast was being prepared. Long tables were lined with stacks of stainless-steel plates, and the aroma of *khichdi*, aloo sabzi, and *kheer* filled the air. Volunteers, some in aprons, others still in their festive saris and kurtas, bustled about, ladling steaming portions of *prasad* onto plates.

Without much discussion, the five women drifted towards the serving counters. The temple announcer had asked for extra hands, and without hesitation, they stepped forward, with a sense of duty—maybe even purpose.

Sugandha tied her *pallu* tightly at her waist and took her place at the station, serving puris. With the rhythmic motion of someone who had done this a thousand times before, she expertly slid two onto each plate, her fingers moving swiftly while her mind wandered. She prayed silently for her son, to keep him safe, to keep him close, to help him understand her heart and that North Indians did not comprehend South Indian sensibilities. As she handed out the warm puris, she recalled how she had done the same at temple events back home, never once thinking she'd do it halfway across the world.

At the next station, Radhika ladled out a generous serving of sabzi. The rich aroma of *hing* and *jeera* filled her nostrils, reminding her of the meals she had once cooked for Virender. She prayed for her son to return, see all she had built, and take pride in their land and roots. She steadied herself with each spoonful she served, repeating in her mind: 'One day, he will understand.'

Sonali, always quick to adapt, had taken charge of handing out bowls of *kheer*. 'Be careful,' she warned a young girl, flashing a warm smile. Her gold bangles jingled softly as she worked. She prayed for Aman to be happy and free, to find love and acceptance, even if she wasn't quite sure how to give it yet. As she served, she noticed a young man with a soft, hesitant smile pick up a bowl, and for a fleeting second, she saw Aman in him.

At the other end, Mona was pouring water into glasses, her usual poise making even this mundane task look elegant. She watched the families settle down—kids chattering, elders eating slowly, couples sharing quiet glances. Her prayer was for Neetu to find love, to be strong, and not to carry the weight of Mona's own heartbreak. As she handed a glass of water to an elderly woman, she blinked back a memory of her mother serving at the gurdwara langar in Malaysia years ago.

Debjyoti, standing beside Supriya, passed plates down the line. She had always believed in *seva*, the act of losing oneself in service. It was a grounding force, a way to push worries aside. Her prayer was heavy yet straightforward—to be of use, to be wanted, to feel that she still had a place in her daughter's world. Watching little boys run around, she secretly prayed that next year she would be here when Supriya came to the temple on Janmashtami!

As the meal progressed, their hands continued to move, their silent prayers blending with the chatter of the temple hall.

After the langar was over, the temple courtyard continued to hum with the murmur of prayers, and the smell of *agarbatti* lingered in the spring air. The women had each come separately, their minds full of preoccupations—sons, daughters, expectations, silences. However, the temple, with its familiar scents of sandalwood and camphor, had a way of loosening tight knots.

Sugandha adjusted her *pallu*, shifting slightly on the temple bench, as she watched the *tulsi* leaves swirl in the water while a small girl tried to scoop them up. Beside her, Radhika muttered a half-prayer, half-complaint under her breath about her son's tardiness in picking her up when their eyes met, and they exchanged a hesitant smile.

'Your child is also here in Seattle?' Radhika asked.

'Yes,' Sugandha said, nodding. 'First time outside India... for me, I mean.'

A brisk voice behind them said, 'I've been here ten days and already craving *rasam* that doesn't taste like tomato juice from a can.' It was Sonali, dressed in a crisp cotton kurta and a vibrant scarf, her bob framing her expressive face. She grinned and slid into the seat beside them.

Mona walked in like she owned the place, oversized sunglasses resting on her head and a scent of Jo Malone lingering behind her. She spotted the trio and raised a perfectly shaped eyebrow. 'I see I'm not the only mother on a mission.'

'And what mission is that?' Debu's warm, slightly teasing voice came from behind her.

They laughed. A laughter that starts as a polite chuckle and unexpectedly turns genuine.

In minutes, stories tumbled out of jet lag and FaceTime arguments, of apartments too small and silences too big, of children who had grown too fast. Something about standing barefoot on the cool temple floor, hearing the chant of mantras in the background, loosened their tongues and softened their edges.

Sonali said, 'Okay, serious question. Are we going to sit here and chat in the temple?'

All five looked at each other. Then Mona wrinkled her nose in theatrical horror.

Debjyoti said, 'There's an Applebee's close by—I walked past it on the way.'

Radhika looked sceptical. 'Applebee? What kind of name is that? Do they serve fruit?'

'Don't worry,' Sonali said, slipping her phone into her kurta pocket. 'They provide precisely what we need—air conditioning, menus in English, and free refills.'

Sugandha hesitated, then smiled. 'Let's go. First time to Applebee's also.'

And just like that, it was a spontaneous, unspoken but unanimous decision. Quick calls were made to the children for a later pickup from Applebee's. Debjyoti asked Supriya to move on while she would go to Applebee's with her new *friends.* The five of them trotted off on their mini-adventure to the fast-food place, which some believed sold fruit.

Applebee's—a necessary evil, selected for its reliable burgers and the welcome absence of prying eyes. The booth was theirs for the night. The conversation? Well, they had only just begun.

Mona ordered sparkling water with lime because hydration was the authentic self-care.

Radhika caught the attention of all Applebee's customers at least once. She looked at the laminated menu with suspicion. '*Yeh sab kuch* fried *kyun hai*? (Why is everything fired?)' she muttered darkly as she sat down with a sigh.

Sonali spoke unusually quickly, tinged with enthusiasm. 'I love how everything in American casual dining smells like melted cheese,' she declared, flopping down beside Radhika.

Sugandha was clutching her handbag as if it held state secrets. She glanced at the menu and exhaled. 'I hope they have rice. I can't keep eating bread all the time,' she murmured, sinking into the booth.

And finally, Debjyoti—cotton sari draped over one shoulder, silver bangles clinking like temple bells. Sliding beside the others, she took in the ambience and declared that she loved it!

Five women, one diner, an evening that would be tucked away in the folds of memory for decades.

The waitress came by, a bright-eyed girl wearing a name tag that read 'Cassidy'. She rattled off the specials—some triple-cheese burger and a dessert featuring flaming marshmallows. The ladies nodded politely, ordered the least intimidating items on the menu, and returned to the business to get to know each other.

Mona stirred her iced tea thoughtfully. 'You know… it's strange. We're all here for our children, but half the time it feels like we're just… waiting for permission to matter in their lives.'

There was a pause.

Radhika let out a low hum. 'True. I came here to convince my son to return home. But he's built a whole world here, and suddenly I feel like an outsider.'

Sonali leaned forward, her voice gentle. 'Isn't that what we taught them, though? To chase dreams? To be independent?'

'But no one tells us how lonely that success can make *us*,' Sugandha said quietly. 'I thought I'd come here, cook for him, take care of him, maybe get to know the girl he's dating….' She trailed off. 'But they're in their bubble. I'm just... floating around the edges.'

Debjyoti smiled softly, the kind that came from seeing a few more seasons of life. 'Maybe that's why we're all meant to meet now.'

Sonali raised her eyebrows. 'Are you saying what I think you're saying?'

Debjyoti chuckled, wrapping her *pallu* tighter around her shoulders. 'Maybe we came here thinking we were just mothers on a mission. But look at us—we're finally asking what *we* want, not just what they need.'

Mona tapped her spoon against the rim of her glass. 'I don't even know what I want anymore. I spent years juggling tiffins, PTA meetings, running to the bank, and suddenly there's all this… silence. No one needs me to pack lunch or sign a form.'

'You're needed,' Radhika said gently. 'Just not in the ways we're used to.'

'Exactly,' Debjyoti nodded. 'And that's the crux of it. We've spent so much time being needed that we forgot how to be. This trip—it's like pressing the reset button.'

Sugandha looked up, something bright flickering behind her eyes. 'You know, I signed up for a pottery class next week, just on a whim. I don't even know if I'll like it. But I figured, maybe it's time to shape something that doesn't start with chopping onions.'

The women laughed.

'I've always wanted to travel to Tuscany,' Sonali admitted, eyes wistful. 'Not with a tour group or family itinerary. Just me, a notebook, and maybe a vineyard or two. But I shelved it—because the timing was never right.'

'Maybe it never will be,' Mona said. 'So we just… go anyway.'

There was a beat of silence. Something warm and unspoken settled over the table.

Cassidy returned with their food, cheerfully placing plates down. 'Here you go, ladies! Let me know if you need anything else.'

As she walked away, Radhika watched her. 'Imagine being twenty again. Everything ahead of you. So many choices.'

'Yes,' Debjyoti smiled. 'But now we have something better, clarity. We've spent decades earning this freedom. The trick is not to waste it waiting.'

Sugandha nodded slowly.

Sonali lifted her glass of water as if it were champagne. 'To return. To reimagine. To Tuscany and pottery and whatever the hell else we feel like.'

They clinked glasses—iced tea, lime water, and half-sipped coffee—not glamorous but perfect.

And a quiet revolution was unfolding—a revolution that does not make headlines but changes lives—one woman at a time, one moment at a time.

As they left the restaurant, they decided to meet again because a friendship had been formed, and each woman felt a kindred spirit in the other. They were all so different, yet they were all the same in a way.

Later at dinner time, Sugandha was in the kitchen, stirring her famous turnip curry. The secret of this curry was that it always tasted better the next day, but no one knew why. The aroma filled the house, as did the low thrum of jazz music that Sharath insisted on playing whenever Sheena came over. Turnip curry paired well with Miles Davis.

Sharath leaned against the counter, his sleeves rolled up as if he were the one cooking. Sheena sat cross-legged on the barstool, sipping kombucha and pretending to enjoy it.

'So, Aunty,' Sheena said, as she expertly tossed mustard seeds into the pan, 'what's this I hear about your new Applebee's girl gang?'

'Gang?' Sugandha blinked. 'It's not a gang. It's not even a club. It's just... a few women I've met. We met at the temple on Janmashtami and then went to Applebee's. There's Mona, a little too chic, Radhika, who's very no-nonsense, Debjyoti, who always wears a Bengali sari, and Sonali... well, she's intense but nice.'

Sheena smiled, intrigued. 'I love this for you. Who's the feisty one? I bet it's Mona.'

Sugandha laughed. 'Mona. She is the type who wears lipstick to the park. Like full red.'

Sharath raised an eyebrow. 'Just... be careful, okay? New friends are great, but people are complex. I don't want you getting caught in anyone's drama.'

'Oh, *thank you*, Sherlock,' Sugandha said dryly. 'I wasn't planning to join a cult. We just talked. We shared a bit. Mostly, we laughed.'

'You don't usually do this,' he replied, gentler now. 'You have your group back home, the walking ladies and the WhatsApp sisters. This is new.'

'I know,' she said, setting the lid on the pot. 'Maybe that's why it matters. These women don't know me from my PTA days or temple committees. They know me now. And they still want to meet again.'

Sheena leaned in. 'Then that's your answer. Aunty, you've spent years looking after others. Your mother, Sharath, that stray cat that used to live behind the washing machine. Now that you're here... go wild. Make friends. Wear red lipstick with Mona. Have wine. Or at least pretend to.'

'I'm not pretending anything,' Sugandha said. 'I'm just... taking it slow.'

Sharath nodded, his face doing that rare thing where concern and pride came together.

Sheena raised her glass of questionable kombucha. 'To new friendships, and turnip curry.'

Sugandha could befriend a pigeon if it looked at her long enough. She also maintained her friendships. Rupa from school was still her friend, although she lived in South Africa and was practising medicine there. They chatted on and off on WhatsApp.

Back home in India, she had a kaleidoscope of friends—walking buddies, WhatsApp buddies, temple ladies, school-gate moms, the lot. They occasionally called her, sharing gossip and recipes and asking about cleaning robots and other gadgets.

The women in this new group were different. They didn't discuss saris or the price of *sabudana*. They argued about therapy, quoted Rumi, and admitted when they felt sad. It was unsettling—and refreshing.

Meeting Mona, especially, gave her a peek into a future version of Sheena—confident, sharply dressed, slightly intimidating, but mostly misunderstood.

Sugandha smiled, suddenly aware that the next chapter of her life might be different from the life she had led so far. She envisioned moving away from the sedate, routine, monotonous existence to something more fun. What exactly, she had no idea.

On the other side of Seattle, Sonali spoke to Rajesh, who had long given up trying to decipher her moods and now scrolled through Instagram with impressive detachment.

'You know what's strange?' she said, still in her Applebee's haze. 'I never thought I'd make new friends after 40.'

Rajesh blinked, surprised she was speaking at all.

Aman, pouring himself coffee, added without looking up, 'Seems strange, but I'm glad you found some friends, Ma.'

Sonali grimaced. 'They're a fun lot, but I don't know how long I can tolerate their conversations. It's good… while it lasts.'

Sonali had always felt like an outsider at the party she was hosting inside her own mind.

A professor by profession and temperament, she was the kind of person others didn't invite to kitty parties. She had learned early on that being smart didn't win you friends—instead, it made people switch tables.

She wasn't sure how she'd ended up at Applebee's with this motley crew, probably out of boredom, or perhaps the secret need to laugh without justifying it with citations.

Elsewhere, Radhika was dissecting the same matter with Vikram, her son, who had never seen his mother socialise with anyone. People in her life were either subordinates, her workers, farmhands, business associates, or potential business associates.

'They're funny, *haan*,' she said, tying her hair into a no-nonsense bun. 'But one of them is so showy, *badi* rich *aur* show-off *lagti hai mujhe* (she seems to be too rich and a show-off to me).'

'*Kaun, Ma?* (Who, Ma?)' Vikram asked, intrigued. This was the most animated she'd been in days.

'Mona,' Radhika declared. 'She's from Delhi. Branded this, branded that. Always lipstick and big hair. *Mujhe aisi* ladies *pasand nahi.* (I don't like such ladies.)'

'*Ek aur hai,* Debjyoti, (There's another one, Debjyoti,)' she added, '*hamesha bimar* type *lagti hai.* (Always looks kind of ill.)'

Vikram smiled. 'Everyone has their faults, Ma. Just be glad you found someone in this country who knows how to pronounce your name.'

Radhika had been a woman on a mission her entire life. Most of her conversations had been with middle-aged men who either underestimated her or tried to overcompensate.

To them, she was a matriarch. Unshakable. Unsmiling. Unfriendly.

She hadn't meant to become friendless. It had just happened over decades of showing strength. Vulnerability had become a luxury she couldn't afford.

Until now, she had found herself talking and laughing with women who knew her very little and accepted her as she is.

Meanwhile, Debjyoti had plumped down onto the sofa in her daughter's neat living room. A large picture of Rabindranath Tagore, which she had painted herself, stared back at her from the wall in front. She had just finished telling her daughter, Supriya, about one of the ladies in her group who reminded her of her loud, lovable Haryanvi college roommate.

Supriya grinned. 'Ma, it's nice you have your own gang.'

'Gang,' Debjyoti laughed, 'like I'm some high schooler again.'

Debjyoti was the social butterfly back home in Kolkata.

She had friends in her music group, the Residents Welfare Association, and even the fish seller knew her by name.

But deep down, she understood that her friendships were often superficial, founded on proximity rather than intimacy. People appreciated her for being polite, not because they genuinely recognised her.

These new women challenged that. They didn't care about her sari pleats or her pronunciation. They argued, laughed, and called her out when she played the victim.

It felt… real.

Mona was facing a similar inquisition at home with her daughter, Neetu.

'Wow, you have friends?' Neetu said, shocked as if her mother had just said she'd joined a punk rock band.

'Why can't I have friends? I'm a very friendly person,' Mona insisted.

Neetu bit into her corn cob and said, 'You are very friendly, if they can get past your Fendi bags and Chanel perfume cloud.'

Mona rolled her eyes. 'We don't talk about bags. We talk about menopause, the meaning of middle age, and men who think they're deep because they own Paulo Coelho books.'

Both mother and daughter burst into laughter.

Mona, for all her glamour, had also walked a lonely road.

She looked the part—impeccable nails, silken scarves, and an enviable collection of perfumes that made strangers turn and inhale. But appearances were like contouring—meant to distract from the mess underneath.

The truth was, her rituals had become tiresome. The women in her family argued over astrology and turmeric face masks. Her school friends had turned into grandmother-shaped alarm clocks, obsessing over calcium tablets and grandchildren. College friends? Lost in retirements, divorces, and existential dilemmas.

In the past year, she had spent more time with her therapist than with her friends. 'You're just someone who enjoys her own company,' the therapist had said.

Mona didn't argue, but she did wonder when self-love had quietly turned into solitude.

The ladies busily discussed their new friends and family over a week. They had already created a WhatsApp group, the first modern sign of friendship, and started exchanging messages about their daily lives. Sonali named their group 'The Rewrite

Circle'. The idea was explained as Reimagine, Rewrite, Reset, Reclaim. She believed that when ladies meet in middle age, they are ready to rewrite their future. Once they pass the big Four O, there is less fear, fewer inhibitions, and more willingness to open up.

It was about to be proven true, very soon.

On one of those rare Seattle afternoons when the sky was an indulgent blue, every item at home said, 'Go outside, woman!'

And so they did. The first text on Sunday was also from Sonali.

Sonali Nadkarni: Ladies, weather alert ☀ sunny Tuesday is coming up in Seattle! Shall we escape from our children and the guilt for a few hours?

Radhika Devi: Arre wah!. Good idea. Green Lake *pe* picnic? It's calm, breezy, *aur* ducks *bhi hain wahan* (and there are ducks too)!"

Mona🍋*:* I'm in! I'll bring lemon rice and tomato chutney. Don't ask how spicy—it's a gamble. 🎲 🔥

Debjyoti: I shall bring chai in my ancient thermos. And folding chairs. We're not 25 years old, girls 😌

Sugandha: I'll bake something sweet. Been experimenting with *nankhatai*. If it fails, we can feed it to squirrels 🐿

Sonali Nadkarni: Love it. I'll do paneer tikka sandwiches and some gossip magazines. Because we're classy like that. 💁

Mona🍋*:* Also, let's wear *non-mom* clothes. No shawls, no aprons, no judgment 😄

Radhika Devi: Can I wear my yoga pants?

Debjyoti: Only if you don't carry your *chhatri* 😆. In Seattle, they recognise a foreigner from a mile away because of their umbrellas!

Sugandha: What time are we meeting?

Radhika Devi: Let's aim for 11.30 a.m. Vikram will share the location 📍 for our picnic spot, which I will then share with everyone.

Mona 🍋: Also, someone please remind me to bring paper plates.

Radhika Devi: Adding it to my checklist.

Debjyoti: This is officially the most exciting thing I've planned in months.

Sonali Nadkarni: Same here. I'll even bring Jake's pink picnic mat. It's pink and might clash with my sense of style, but it's worth it.

See you all on Tuesday. Food, fresh air, and fabulous women—what more could we ask for?

Mona 🍋: Someone, please bring tissues. We'll cry, laugh, and wipe curry all in one go 🥲 😂

Radhika had discovered the perfect picnic spot, thanks to some help from Vikram—a quiet patch by Green Lake, where tall trees provided dappled shade and the breeze carried the scents of pine and fresh grass. They arrived like a caravan of possibilities, each woman clutching something wrapped in foil or carried in steel dabbas that had withstood generations.

'We've officially turned into our mothers,' Debjyoti said, pulling out a thermos of masala chai and neatly stacked boxes of paneer tikka sandwiches brought by Sonali.

'I brought lemon rice,' Mona scoffed, laying out a faded floral bedsheet. Sugandha, always the quiet one, unveiled a box of ghee-laced *nankhatai* cookies like she was smuggling joy. 'I baked these last night. They may or may not be edible.'

Debjyoti bit into one and closed her eyes dramatically. 'You could open a bakery. Call it *Menopause and Muffins*.'

The women howled with laughter, drawing the curious glances of joggers and a toddler who stopped mid-tantrum to stare.

Blankets spread, food unpacked, shoes kicked off—they sat in a circle, legs crossed or stretched out, plates balanced on laps, the lake shimmering beside them like nature's Instagram filter. The folding chairs that Debjyoti had brought were still in the boot of her car!

'So this,' Sonali said, sipping chai, 'is The Rewrite Circle.'

Radhika was pouring water into paper cups with the grace of someone who'd hosted a hundred kitty parties and a dozen weddings. 'Yes, a circle of newfound friends—after having lived for more than half a century!'

They laughed again, that effortless, shoulder-shaking sort of laughter that occurs when no one is pretending.

'I like the name,' said Mona, adjusting her sunglasses. 'It sounds like we're editing our pasts.'

'Or rewriting our second innings,' said Sugandha, reaching for a biscuit.

Sonali raised her cup. 'Cheers to that. And fewer expectations. Also, my son now sends me one-word texts, whereas his friend sends me lengthy messages. That's character development, right?'

'I get full sentences,' said Radhika smugly. 'Mostly instructions. "Ma, don't open the oven." "Ma, don't talk to Alexa." As if I'm a five-year-old with access to matches.'

'Are you still scared of Alexa?' Sonali teased, having freshly acquired better knowledge about its uses.

'I don't talk to things that glow and listen silently. That's not a servant, that's a spy.'

They all burst into laughter. A group of women from different corners of India and walks of life, now stitched together by second chances, late-night calls, and shared nostalgia.

Sonali looked around the circle and smiled. 'Who would've thought?'

Debjyoti nodded. 'The Rewrite Circle. Not bad for a bunch of women who were told our best chapters were behind us.'

They laughed again.

Birds fluttered nearby, the occasional paddleboarder glided past, and the conversations swayed between nostalgia and dreams. Middle age is the only life stage where memories and planning coexist!

'I never thought I'd feel this… alive,' Sugandha admitted. 'After all these years of running a household like a boot camp, I forgot what it was like just to sit. Eat. Breathe.'

Mona lay back on the blanket, sunglasses perched on her nose. 'It's like we've been defrosted. Slowly. And deliciously.'

Someone passed around the cookies again. Someone else found music on their phone.

'*Khwab ho tum ya koi haqeeqat*,' Kishore crooned, and each lady thought he sang just for her. They smiled, they sang, they shared.

No big revelations. No tearful breakthroughs. Just women, food, and the realisation that *this* was living. Perhaps even the best part of it.

As the sun dipped lower, casting golden halos on the water, Debjyoti raised her paper cup.

'To all the things we thought were behind us… and all the joys we've just begun to claim.'

They toasted with water and crumbs, and everything unsaid between them.

And for a brief, glimmering moment, the world stood still—just enough for them to feel it. Freedom. Friendship. And finally, themselves.

Over the next month, The Rewrite Circle met again and again—at cafés, on park benches, in each other's kitchens, where parathas, pickles, and banana bread shared the same table without judgment. The meetings were casual at first, with chai, idle talk, book swaps, and shared grocery runs—but gradually, without ceremony, the conversations deepened. Sugandha opened up about her mother's declining memory. Mona confessed that she sometimes stood in her café after closing time to remember who she was before she became everyone's caregiver. Sonali showed them a poem she hadn't shared with anyone in years. And Radhika, always the composed one, let them see the edges of her loneliness. Trust arrived like spring in

Seattle—slow, hesitant, then all at once. They began to call each other not just for plans, but for silences, opinions, recipes, and comfort. The circle tightened.

On a rare sunny afternoon in Seattle, at Radhika's apartment, The Rewrite Circle gathered. The curtains were drawn wide open, allowing light to spill onto the polished floor. The dining table had been pushed back slightly to make space for cushions and chatter. A faint sizzle emanated from the kitchen where Radhika was in her element, flipping aloo parathas like a professional, her dupatta neatly tucked at her waist.

Sonali arrived first, holding a tub of yoghurt. '*Dahi*,' she announced dramatically. 'Because we're civilised people and not savages who eat parathas with ketchup.'

Mona followed, carrying a Spotify playlist and a box of store-bought *gulab jamuns*. 'Don't judge me,' she said, slipping off her shoes. 'I was too lazy to make dessert. But look, they're soaked!'

Soon, Sugandha walked in, a paperback sticking out of her bag, and her eyeliner perfect. 'This place smells like Sheena made something,' she sighed, inhaling deeply. 'Look, Mona, the eyeliner you taught me to apply!' She blinked her eyes. Mona cooed in appreciation!

They sat cross-legged on the floor with steel plates in hand—parathas stacked high, pickle glinting in the sunlight, laughter bubbling over between bites. Radhika moved around fussing, placing water, chutney, tissues, until Mona pulled her down. 'Enough, queen. Sit. This is not your Rohtak *ki shaadi* buffet.'

They ate, talked, teased, and let the afternoon melt into golden quiet.

Almost abruptly, Mona raised her glass high and grinned. 'Alaska.'

Sugandha blinked. 'What?'

'Let's go! The five of us,' Mona sat up with excitement shining in her eyes.

Radhika looked at them, a spark igniting behind her practical eyes. 'You're serious.'

'Why not? I've always wanted to see the Northern Lights,' Sonali said.

'*Chalte hain,* (Let's go,)' Debjyoti said. 'We can think of it as… a pilgrimage of a different kind. One where we figure out who we are when we're not someone's mother, someone's wife, someone's emergency contact.'

They sat silently for a moment, the idea floating above the bowl of *dahi*.

Then Sugandha, of all people, laughed. 'Only if we find a place with hot water and vegetarian food.'

'Deal,' Mona said, raising her glass.

Five women. One plan. No permission slips needed.

Much later that night, they found themselves gathered at Mona's house. Neetu was travelling, so Mona was by herself. Nursing cups of masala chai, shoes kicked off, and sari *pallus* and dupattas loosened in a way that signalled they were finally comfortable. They were staying over. All girls' pyjama party like never before!

Radhika exhaled, staring out the window at the cityscape. 'We were serious, weren't we?' she murmured.

Mona stretched her legs out on the ottoman, looking too pleased. 'Absolutely.'

Sugandha hesitated. 'But… do we mean it?' She gestured vaguely, as if the notion of Alaska was too big, too wild to fit inside the room's four walls. 'We joke about these things. And then life happens. And then we… don't.'

Sonali leaned forward, fingers wrapped around her warm mug. 'But life *already* happened,' she said. 'We raised our children. We did everything expected of us. This… this is something no one expects. Isn't that the point?'

A thoughtful silence followed.

Debjyoti smiled, settling her cup down. 'I think this is the part where we either talk ourselves out of it or start looking up flights.'

Mona grabbed her phone with a decisive air, tapping her screen with exaggerated enthusiasm. 'You are right, Debu!' Mona looked at her intently. The group had found Debjyoti to be a tongue-twisting name and had shortened it to Debu. Debu, of course, loved it because that's what everyone had called her in her childhood, and now very few people still called her that. Being Debu had changed her personality. 'Fairbanks,' Mona announced. 'If we're going to see the Northern Lights, we do it properly.'

The room shifted. Sugandha sat up straighter. Radhika tilted her head in consideration. Sonali let out the smallest gasp.

The idea was no longer hypothetical.

The idea was real.

The next morning dawned with nervous energy usually reserved for job interviews or doctor's appointments. But instead of waiting for results, the women were about to drop a bombshell: *We're going to Alaska. Without you. On purpose.*

Radhika went first. She spoke to Vikram just before his morning meeting started.

'Alaska?' he repeated slowly, like she'd said she was climbing Everest.

'Yes,' she said, trying to keep her voice steady. 'With friends. For a few days. It's not that far from Seattle, right?'

He was quiet for a beat too long. 'Ma… are you okay?'

'I'm *fine*,' she snapped. 'Can't a woman take a trip without sounding like she's run away from home?'

'Of course! No—I mean—it's cool. Unexpected. But cool.' Then, after a pause, 'Should I buy you some thermals? And maybe a good neck pillow? Also, Ma, make sure that all of you carry your travel and health insurance papers. You might not have Internet connectivity, so it would be better to take prints. Please ask your friends to do this too. I shall take prints for you.'

Radhika smiled. Her boy had always been practical.

Sugandha waited until her son and Sheena were back from work. Then, she joined them at the dining table, acting casually as she folded his laundry.

'I'm going to Alaska next week,' she said, placing a pair of socks on his bed.

Her son looked up mid-scroll. 'With whom?'

'With... Mona Aunty, Radhika Aunty, and the others,' she said. 'We thought we'd see the Northern Lights.'

Sheena beamed. 'That sounds amazing! Good for you, Aunty!'

Her son blinked, uncertain. 'Is this a... tour package thing? Like one of those desi aunty groups in matching jackets?'

Sugandha bristled. 'No jackets. No matching. Just... women. Making our own decisions.'

Sheena reached over and high-fived her. Her son mumbled something about safety and looked deeply betrayed, as if his mother had gone rogue. But Sugandha felt something loosen inside her, like the first button of a blouse on a summer day. The spontaneous reaction from Sheena warmed her heart.

Sonali dropped the news over brunch with her husband, son, and Jake.

'You're going where?' Aman laughed, his fork suspended in mid-air.

'Alaska. With the girls. Just us,' she said, slicing her pancake neatly. 'We've booked tickets.'

Her husband looked alarmed. 'But what about your lectures?'

'I've taught enough about women in history,' she said dryly. 'I'm going to live a bit of it.'

Aman raised his mimosa. 'I love this for you, Ma.'

'Exactly,' she said, clinking her glass against his. 'Your turn to be surprised for once.'

Debjyoti didn't ask her daughter for permission, but she informed her.

'You're really going to Alaska, *sotti* (really)?' Supriya asked, looking up with a smile that was half admiration, half disbelief.

Debjyoti nodded, adding a dash of sugar. 'Yes. With the ladies. We've booked a cabin near a lake. I won't exert, I promise.'

Supriya walked over and leaned on the counter, eyebrows raised. 'Wow. You people have become... adventurers. Can I come?'

Debu smiled gently. 'Not this time, darling. This one's just for us. We're going to talk without filters, cry if we feel like it, dance badly, and sleep in wool socks. You'd hate it.'

'I'd love it,' Supriya said, mock-sulking.

'I know. But you'll have your own trips. With your friends. *Amake shudhu mukto kore dao* (Just set me free).'

There was a pause, soft and affectionate. Debu asking to be freed? Supriya's eyes filled with tears.

'You've changed, Ma,' Supriya said finally. 'In a good way.'

Debu looked out the window, where the first slant of spring sunlight kissed the windowsill. 'I think I've just come back to myself.'

They sipped in silence, the kind only love can fill.

Mona texted Neetu, knowing her daughter wouldn't reply for at least six hours.

Mona: Going to Alaska next week. Girls' trip. Northern Lights. No boys allowed.

Six hours later:

Neetu: Wait. What?? Who are you, and what have you done with my mother?

Neetu: Also—WELL DONE.

Neetu: Don't forget moisturiser. That Arctic air is brutal.

Mona smirked. Her daughter would never admit it, but she was impressed. And Mona? She was already looking for snow-proof, Instagrammable boots.

By nightfall, all five women had survived their family debriefs. They regrouped in their WhatsApp group, The Rewrite Circle, and sent emojis ranging from 🛫 to ❄️ to 💃.

They were not daydreaming anymore.

They *were going.*

CHAPTER 5

The Edge of Everything

The wind in Fairbanks had teeth.

It greeted them, biting, persistent, and unforgettable. As the five women stepped out of the tiny regional airport, bundled in puffers and scarves that still felt foreign on their bodies, a collective gasp rose from them.

'*Ye kya tha?* (What was that?)' Sugandha muttered, hugging her handbag like a child. Every time she was with her new friends, Sugandha started speaking in a smattering of Hindi, as much as she could muster. She would translate the words in her mind, and so her speech seemed deliberate and slow.

'Welcome to Alaska,' Sonali said, her breath already fogging up her sunglasses.

Mona threw her arms wide open, twirling once. 'This is *bloody brilliant*! We did it! Look at us!' Anyone would look at her many times. She looked stunning in her blue jeans and purple high-neck sweater. A black puffer jacket with a white fleece lining complemented her look, and the Celine sunglasses added to her appeal.

Debu, serene as ever, adjusted her muffler. 'We're not tourists,' she said with a smile. 'We're pilgrims.'

Debu had discarded her cotton saris and was now dressed in trousers and sweatshirts borrowed from Supriya's closet. Supriya took personal interest in packing the clothes for her mother because 'Anyway, they don't fit me anymore,' she grinned mischievously. Throughout the flight, Debu clutched Mona's hand, and Mona patted it like she understood her fear.

Their Airbnb was a wooden cabin nestled in a tranquil pine forest. It featured a fireplace, creaky floorboards, and a suspicious raccoon family roaming in the courtyard. The moment they stepped inside, bags were flung, boots came off, and heaters were switched on.

Radhika, who'd insisted on bringing homemade *laddus* just in case, unpacked them ceremoniously.

'Emergency food,' she announced. 'Don't ask questions.'

They giggled like schoolgirls. Women with cold noses and warm hearts, trying to remember how to be silly again, not five middle-aged Indian women with passports, prescriptions, and polite reputations.

'Call dibs on the bed *not* next to the heater!' Mona shouted, lugging her floral suitcase and kicking off her snow boots. 'I refuse to wake up medium rare.'

'Sonali's already there,' Sugandha called from the loft, peeking down, cheeks flushed from the climb. 'She said she's claiming the mountain view for "poetic reflection".'

'*Arre*,' Radhika said, settling her dupatta, '*Koi chai banao yaar* (Someone please make some tea). My bones are still somewhere over Anchorage.'

'I'll make it,' Debu announced, pulling down her hoodie. 'But don't judge, okay? It's from a bag. I didn't come to Alaska to grate ginger.'

The kettle whistled as laughter rose. Sonali turned on music—some 90s Bollywood hit—and suddenly Mona was doing a full-on Govinda step in her thermal leggings. Debu joined her, shimmying dramatically with her hoodie sliding over her eyes.

'Ladies, control!' Radhika scolded, grinning despite herself.

'You're next, madam!' Debu said, pulling her in. 'Come on, *thoda* Alaska *hilao* (shake some Alaska)!'

'Forget glaciers,' Sonali giggled, filming the moment. 'We're melting the ice with our hips, and remember, hips don't lie.'

They danced and sang and let their hair down, including Radhika, who had never even heard of Shakira in her life!

That night, they gathered outside, wrapped in mismatched layers, necks craned upward.

The sky was clear, and the auroras were late.

'Typical,' Mona said. 'The one thing that brought us all the way here decides to ghost us.'

'Give it time,' Debu said gently. 'Everything worth seeing takes its own sweet time.'

They sipped hot chocolate from camping mugs. The stars above seemed so close that they felt like they could reach out and touch them. The silence was not empty—it was alive and waiting.

And then—

A shimmer. A green thread weaving across the sky.

Sugandha gasped. Sonali blinked back tears. Radhika held her breath. Mona stopped talking.

The Northern Lights weren't dancing. They were whispering.

You're still here. You still matter. You are allowed to begin again.

No one spoke. No one needed to. The lights twirled across the night sky as time loosened its grip.

They stood there long after the cold began to ache in their bones, until it stopped hurting.

Inside the cabin later, huddled under quilts, the conversation turned.

'I forgot how small we are,' Radhika whispered. 'And how free that can feel.'

'It's like the universe said to us, shut up and feel something,' Mona muttered, eyes glassy.

Sugandha smiled. 'Maybe this is what it means to be alive after 40. To break your own rules.'

'Or rewrite them,' said Sonali.

Debu nodded. 'To not wait for permission.'

That night, they slept like they hadn't in years. Unfinished, unsure, and unburdened.

The calamity struck on the second night after the auroras.

The group had just returned from a mild hike near Chena Hot Springs, their spirits high and their cheeks pink from the cold. However, Sonali had been quiet, not withdrawn, just… watchful. She was smiling, yes, but now and then, she discreetly pressed a hand to her chest.

Back at the cabin, Mona busied herself preparing Maggi in a makeshift saucepan while Radhika tended to the fireplace, determined to coax the stubborn flames to behave. Sugandha and Debu curled up with mugs of ginger tea, exchanging stories as their voices grew warmer and more relaxed.

Then, Sonali stood.

Too quickly.

She froze.

Her hand flew to her chest.

'I… give me a minute,' she whispered just before her knees buckled.

Mona dropped the ladle.

'Sonali?'

She never hit the floor—four sets of hands caught her just in time.

Then came the blur of hours.

No phone signal. Snow-blocked roads. The emergency GPS device buried somewhere in Mona's suitcase.

Debu, steady despite the chaos, took charge. 'We need to keep her warm. Talk to her. Don't let her drift.'

Sugandha clutched Sonali's hand, her own trembling. 'This is my fault. I made her climb those rocks. She didn't want to—'

'She didn't *say* anything,' Mona snapped. 'Why didn't she *say* anything?'

'She never does,' Radhika muttered. 'That's the problem with women like her. They suffer quietly and make it look glamorous.'

Sonali's eyelids fluttered. A faint smile. 'Rude,' she whispered. 'But fair.'

A laugh—sharp, shaky, tinged with fear and relief.

Three hours later, after Mona hiked half a mile to find a neighbour with a radio signal, the paramedics finally arrived. Sonali was airlifted to a hospital in Fairbanks. The diagnosis was minor angina. Not a heart attack—but a warning. A wake-up call. Thanks to Vikram's reminder, all of them had their insurance papers. Mona fished them out of Sonali's luggage, and at least they didn't have to worry about hospital bills.

The antiseptic smell in the hospital was sharp enough to jolt Mona's sinuses into alertness. She stood at the reception desk, eyes darting between the clock and the double doors the paramedics had wheeled Sonali through twenty minutes ago.

Radhika paced near the vending machine, fists clenched. Her hiking boots squeaked with every about-turn. 'They should've let me carry her. It would've been faster than that airlift.'

Debu, meanwhile, had found the nurses' station and was in full research mode. 'Look,' she told a nurse patiently typing notes, 'you're doing great, but minor angina can still indicate coronary artery spasms. Any beta-blockers prescribed yet? She's allergic to atenolol, by the way.'

The nurse blinked. 'And you are…?'

'I am Debjyoti,' she grinned, flashing a badge of zero authority but absolute sincerity.

Behind the doors, Sonali was propped up on a bed, an IV trailing from her wrist. She looked pale, but she was smiling. When the cardiologist walked in, she sat up straighter. 'Doctor, I understand this is not a full-blown myocardial infarction,' she began, her voice smooth. 'But we need a proper lipid profile and perhaps a stress echo?'

The doctor raised an eyebrow. 'You have a medical background?'

'All of us in India have a bit of it,' she replied with a faint smile.

Out in the hallway, Mona was on the phone with her bank. 'Yes, wire the emergency funds now to my account. No, I'm not giving you my OTP again. You know who I am, right? Great.'

Moments later, she confidently marched back toward the nurse's desk.

Radhika returned with three bottles of water and a sandwich she'd bullied from the vending machine. 'Eat something.'

Sonali smiled as her friends trickled into the room.

'So,' she said, looking around, 'we make a good emergency team, no?'

Mona sat down and flicked an invisible speck off her coat. 'Remind me to get you a panic button that texts *all* of us next time.'

Debu was already reading her cholesterol numbers.

And Radhika pulled up a chair, arms crossed. 'Good thing you're okay. But next time your heart tries to pull a stunt like this, it will have to answer to *me*.'

Back at the cabin that night, silence stretched long and heavy.

Mona was the first to break it. 'I've been pretending,' she admitted, staring into her untouched cup of tea. 'Pretending that if I keep making noise, keep buying things, keep pushing… I won't have to feel how lonely I am.'

Sugandha's voice was barely above a whisper. 'I came here thinking I'd find freedom. And now I feel… terrified of what it means. Especially alone.'

Radhika exhaled. 'All these years, I thought I was in control. Land. Labour. Life. But watching Sonali lying there… all I could think was—what if this is the last chapter, and we're still writing it like it's the prologue?'

Debu, steady as ever, folded her hands around her mug. 'This isn't the end. Nor is it the beginning. This is the middle. The messy, brilliant middle.'

Sonali smiled from the far corner of the bed. Middle… just like the middle seat, the middle age, the middle years!

No one spoke after that. They just sat there, bound by a terrifying truth.

The next morning, Debu was quiet—too quiet. Her silence carried weight, making the others glance at her, their concern growing with each passing minute.

She had been steady through Sonali's episode—boiling water, propping pillows, murmuring reassurances. But now, with Sonali stable and out of danger, she sat hunched near the window, palm pressed flat against her chest. Not in pain. In memory.

Sugandha noticed it first. 'You're not okay,' she said gently.

Debjyoti gave a tight smile. 'I haven't been "okay" since I was nine.'

The others turned to look at her.

'I had open-heart surgery as a child,' she said, voice steady but distant. 'A hole in my heart. They said I was lucky to survive it.' She shrugged, and Mona gasped. 'Wait. What?'

'I've lived with this ticking clock inside me ever since—tick-tock, be careful. Don't get too excited. Don't exert yourself. Don't travel too far. Don't get too happy.'

She exhaled, eyes drifting toward the snow-draped trees outside.

Debu took a slow sip of her now-cold tea. 'So when we talked about Alaska that night at your place, Mona, I thought—well, if I'm going to take one reckless chance in my life, let it be this one.'

Sonali, still pale but sitting up now, met her eyes. 'You're braver than all of us.'

Debu shook her head. 'No. I've just lived with the expiration date always in sight. This trip… it's the first time I've felt like maybe I can outrun it. Even if just for a while.'

They sat quietly, taking in Debu's reality.

After what seemed like eternity, Radhika murmured, 'I've spent so long fighting to keep things alive—land, crops, my business… even my son's ties to India. But I never stopped to think about what it truly means to live.'

Unusually quiet, Mona ran a fingertip along the rim of her mug. 'Maybe we all came here to be brave in a different way. And maybe we needed a little fear to understand what courage even means.'

Sugandha, eyes shining, wiped at her cheeks. 'I thought I was just visiting my son. I didn't realise I was visiting a version of myself I'd forgotten existed.'

No one spoke after that.

But something had shifted.

Not just between them, but within them.

They sat together in a loose circle—knees tucked in, bodies draped in blankets, laughter softened into murmurs.

The fire had burned to a lazy orange glow, flickering softly, as if unwilling to fade completely. Outside, snowflakes whispered against the windows.

Mona stretched, raising an eyebrow. 'Alright. Confession time.'

Debu smirked, pulling her blanket tighter around her shoulders. 'You first.'

Mona exhaled heavily. 'Fine. I didn't just come to check on Neetu. I came because… she no longer needs me. And that terrified me. I thought if I showed up, maybe I'd find something—some proof that I still mattered.'

Radhika, who had been stirring the embers with a poker, nodded without looking up. 'Same. I wanted to drag my son back to India. I thought he was drifting too far. But maybe… I was the one who didn't want to be left behind.'

Sugandha exhaled, voice quiet. 'My son told me he's in love with a North Indian girl. That broke me in ways I'm ashamed to admit. I came to see if I could accept her. If I could… let go of that old wound.'

Sonali, pale but stronger now, smiled softly. 'I think Aman is gay.'

The room stilled.

She took a deep breath. 'I always thought I was modern. Open-minded. I was proud of my multicultural upbringing. But when I observed Jake and him, my world shattered. Not because I didn't love him—of course I do—but because I realised, I didn't understand him *fully*. I need to learn. To listen. To understand him—and if I'm honest, to understand myself.'

Debu's eyes were reflective, and she shifted in her chair. 'And I came because I've spent my whole life preparing for the end. But I thought to myself—if you want to see the lights in the sky before you go, you'd better move. So I moved. My daughter is pregnant, and I am worried that I might pass on my congenital defect to her children. I am scared.'

The silence that followed wasn't empty—it was full, weighted, shared.

Then Sugandha sniffled abruptly and cleared her throat. 'Do you remember that old Lata song? From *Anari*?'

Mona's eyes lit up. '*Woh chand khila, woh tare hanse…*' she sang, slightly off-key but without hesitation.

And just like that, the others joined in.

Mugs were raised in mock toasts. Harmonies clashed and blended. Radhika clapped off-beat, laughing at herself. Debu hummed with her eyes closed, face tilted skyward. Sonali wiped a tear but didn't hide it.

The song faded.

No one rushed to fill the silence.

Instead, they leaned back, listening to the soft wind outside and the occasional creak of the wood as the cabin settled around them.

Sonali smiled absently, holding her mug close. 'This is our story for the first time in our lives.'

And outside, unseen by all, the sky shimmered faintly with green—the Northern Lights rising again, as if in quiet agreement.

The morning mist cloaked the cabin, blurring the edges of the pine trees. The sun started its shy ascent, casting peach-tinted streaks across the snow-covered landscape. It was September—early enough for winter's whispers, late enough for the trees to blush gold. It was also the best time to be here.

Inside the cabin, the fire in the wood stove had dimmed to a warm amber glow, occasionally crackling as if stretching after a good nap.

Radhika was already outside. In a grey thermal top and neon-orange snow boots—unnecessarily loud but very "her"—she swung an axe with mechanical precision, splitting logs. Her breath puffed in little clouds, her hair tied in a no-nonsense bun—nature, wood, muscle—her holy trinity.

Inside, Mona padded around the kitchen, made up and ready. She poured almond milk into a French press with the flair of a Parisian barista. 'Ladies, coffee is five minutes away from being divine. Debu, don't use that cup, it doesn't match the tray.' She smiled naughtily.

Debu, who had crashed on the couch after an intense late-night research session, groaned and rolled onto her side. Her laptop was open, tabs multiplying like bunnies—Mayo Clinic, WebMD, and a suspicious Reddit thread on turmeric's effect on heart health.

'Does anyone know where the HDMI cable went? I need to project Sonali's cholesterol trajectory on the TV for a quick discussion.'

Mona shot her a look. 'It's 6.00 a.m., who do you want to talk to?'

'My doctor in India,' Debu replied.

Sonali, meanwhile, was on the porch, wrapped in a thick shawl, sitting cross-legged on a rocking chair with a cup of warm lemon water. Her fingers danced over her phone, half-dictating, half-typing a blog post: 'When your heart reminds you to listen—to snow, to stillness, to your own breath.' She paused, then deleted it. Too dramatic. She tried again: 'What nearly gave out, ironically, gave in—and now I'm here, learning to sit still before my heart makes me lie down.' She had begun befriending the gadgets around her.

The raccoon family sauntered into the courtyard, looking for food. Sonali looked up and smiled, too seasoned now to be surprised. 'Good morning, guys. You and I—we're both survivors.'

Radhika swung the last log onto the stack and came inside, cheeks flushed. 'Why are you all acting like we're in a spa retreat? We've got to clean out the compost toilet before leaving.'

Mona sipped her coffee and looked horrified. 'That is a sentence I deeply regret hearing before caffeine.'

Sonali chuckled. 'I'll supervise. From a respectful distance.'

Debu, bleary-eyed but determined, held up a mug. 'To surviving heart scares, raccoon sightings, and Radhika's compost crusade.' It was common in cabins to rely on composting or outhouse arrangements. It's part of the rugged charm and practicality of off-grid Alaska living. And they had done it!

They clinked mugs—ceramic, chipped, mismatched—and the cabin, with all its creaks and quirks, seemed to exhale with them.

The Rewrite Circle was real—it was no longer just a WhatsApp group. Mona started to sing an old Carpenters song… 'We've only just begun...'

The pact was made—not loud or dramatic, but in that quiet, unshakeable way that specific promises take root.

By evening, the cold had intensified. The air was thin and crisp, and the stars stood out sharply against the vast, dark expanse of the sky. The cabin door remained open, offering an invitation to something greater than themselves.

The women stood on the porch, the chill biting at their cheeks, but none of them moved to go inside. They were all looking up.

And then, it began.

At first, it was just a whisper of light—a faint green flicker, like an artist's first hesitant stroke against black velvet. Then, as if the sky had decided to unveil a long-held secret, the light grew. It pulsed, stretched, and shifted into waves of emerald and violet, then gold. The sky danced, shimmering with impossible hues, as if the stars themselves had stepped back to make room for something grander.

Radhika gasped, pressing a hand to her mouth. 'It's…. It's like the sky is alive.'

Mona, eyes wide, barely breathed.

Sonali was lost in something more profound. 'It's more than beautiful. It feels like… a promise.'

Sugandha blinked, her eyes glistening, though she did not look away. 'A promise that we can still change.'

Debu let out a slow breath, the moment unravelling something within her. 'I feel like I've just seen the universe stretch its arms wide and say—there is more.'

The five of them stood there, silent and bound. The Northern Lights shimmered above like a living, breathing force, shifting, expanding, and dissolving. Each carried thoughts too vast to name, yet their weight—the truth of them—kept them united in a way nothing else ever had.

This sight was a reminder that they, too, were shifting.

As the lights gradually faded, leaving the sky in peaceful stillness, a different kind of confidence settled within them. They had recognised their own potential shining through each other.

Back inside the cabin, warmth enfolded them, yet no one spoke immediately. There was no need. The silence was filled with understanding.

Finally, Sonali spoke, her voice quiet but steady. 'We've spent our whole lives afraid to be anything beyond what's expected. But tonight… it feels like we have permission to be more. To be everything we've hidden inside.'

Radhika nodded, the spark of something new glimmering in her eyes. 'We've been waiting for the world to change. But maybe it's us. Maybe *we* are the ones who needed to shift.'

Sugandha reached for her cup, her grip firm. 'Then let's give ourselves the space to do that. No more fear. No more guilt. No more shrinking.'

Mona smiled, slow and sure, a decision settling within her. 'Let's take the risk. Let's see where this journey goes—without apology.'

This wasn't about Alaska anymore. This was about *them*.

The Northern Lights had come and gone. But the change had already begun.

And now, they would carry that light within them.

CHAPTER 6

The Makeover

Sugandha

Sugandha sat cross-legged on the thick rug by the fireplace, gently running her fingers through a bowl of dry lavender Mona had left in a wooden tray. The warmth of the room, the smell of chai steeping, the soft hum of Sonali and Mona singing a Lata Mangeshkar tune somewhere reminded her of home. And yet, it was not.

This was not Machilipatnam, Hyderabad, or any railway colony where walls were thin, and life was loud. This was Alaska. And somehow, she had ended up here.

She spent most of her life believing that her job was to preserve culture, family rituals, recipes, values, and the order of things. She made *pulihora* from scratch even if no one asked. She celebrated *Varalakshmi Vratham* even if her husband barely noticed. She tried to raise her son, Sharath, to speak Telugu, fold his hands to elders, and keep to his 'own kind'.

And now, here she was.

A mother of a young man who cooked his own meals, worked in Seattle, and loved a girl who wasn't Telugu. Who wasn't even South Indian.

She smiled when Sheena called her 'Aunty' in a singsong tone with no respect. But inside, Sugandha had burned. Not out of hatred, no—she was not cruel. But out of fear.

Fear that her son would forget his roots. That she would become unnecessary.

But these days, after their trip, after the conversations, the tears, and the laughter, something had changed.

Sitting here, her hands fragrant with lavender, Sugandha finally allowed herself to whisper what she had never said aloud.

'He has to live his life. Not the life I imagined for him.'

She pressed her palm over her eyes and let the sting pass.

She thought of her own past—the boy from her youth, Sanjay Chopra, the one her father had separated her from. Maybe if she had been allowed to choose, she wouldn't have spent so many years mourning in silence. Wasn't she behaving like her father dictating the unspoken terms of how to lead his life? She still bore this grudge against her father and often wondered if Sanjay and she would have remained friends and met again.

She didn't want to do that to Sharath.

She thought of Sheena—sharp, modern, outspoken. Everything Sugandha wasn't. But perhaps everything Sharath needed.

She smiled suddenly—a strange smile, part pain, part peace.

'*Atanini avvanivvu, Sugandha*,' she whispered to herself in Telugu. 'Let him become.'

When she returned, she would tell him that he had her blessing and that she would always love him, even if he danced to different music now.

And more than that, she would begin learning to love her life again.

Maybe she'd take English classes at the local women's college back home. Perhaps she'd go on the temple tour of Tamil Nadu she'd once put off. Maybe she'd teach young girls how to cook traditional Andhra recipes—not because culture must be preserved, but because it brings joy.

She rose, stretched her limbs, and walked over to the window, where the lights still shimmered. She gently pressed her palm against the cold glass.

'Be happy, Sharath,' she said aloud. 'I'm learning how to be happy, too.'

The following morning, as the others packed, Sugandha sat alone in the porch nook. A blue notebook rested open in her lap—a gift from Debu, with a note tucked inside: 'To new pages, and the courage to write them your way.'

Sugandha had never kept a diary. But today, words flowed.

She wrote down three things:

1. Speak to Sharath—and really listen.

2. Invite Sheena to stay during Sankranti—include her. If she's willing, teach her and learn from her as well.

3. Start the Telugu-meets-Hindi cooking club.

Yes, that last one had been a joke at first. Radhika had laughed and said, 'Only you, Sugandha, can make someone feel ashamed for putting *jeera* in tamarind rice.' But now… it didn't feel like a joke.

She imagined a small group back in her colony—women from different parts of India, married into the South or born there—who felt left out and tried to find a common ground in cooking.

She would host it monthly. It would be open-hearted and nothing fancy. It would be a way to break down her own walls. She might even call it *Vaṇṭagadi* and *Rasoi* (kitchen).

And she would start with herself.

She picked up her phone, staring at the contact that had once given her so much anxiety: *Sheena Singh.*

After a pause, she typed:

'When you and Sharath are free, let's cook something together. I want to learn how you make your *rajma*.'

She hesitated before hitting send.

Then she did.

A small message. But a giant leap.

As she looked again at the snow-covered horizon, Sugandha realised something surprising. She no longer felt small or lost in this vast country. She felt… open.

She no longer needed to define herself solely by her fears or her roots. She could cultivate new ones. She moved over to the table where a vase of dried flowers served as decoration. She took out a small forget-me-not and tucked it into her hair. Mallepuvvu, she thought and smiled, recalling her grandmother, mother, and all the ladies who had shaped her life.

She closed her notebook and whispered with conviction, 'I will not be scared of change. Not anymore.'

Radhika

Radhika had always moved with purpose. Even now, as she crunched along the icy path behind the lodge, her steps were confident and determined. Snow may have covered the world around her, but she carried the warmth of harvest fields, the scent of damp earth after the monsoon, and a no-nonsense practicality.

And yet, she had never felt smaller than she had the previous night—beneath that vast sky ablaze with dancing lights, amid four women who had seen through her silence.

She hadn't cried. Radhika Devi didn't cry. But she was different now.

Mona and Sonali whispered inside the room so as not to disturb the others asleep. Radhika sat on a log bench, pulled her thick shawl tighter around her, and watched the breath rise from her mouth. She had faced droughts, widowhood, greedy relatives, and the indifference of a son who once promised to return and never did. Sitting in this strange, frozen land, she wondered if holding on so tightly was doing more harm than good.

Was it truly wrong for her son to want a different life? Had she turned her grief into a chain that bound him?

When Radhika heard Mona's light, full-bellied laughter, something stirred within her. She recalled their conversation last night, when Debjyoti shared about her surgery, Sonali shared about her son, and Sugandha talked about her fears. Radhika felt an unfamiliar ache blossom in her chest.

Loneliness.

She rubbed her palms together, deep in thought. Sugandha's voice interrupted the silence. 'You're up early.'

'I don't sleep much. It's a habit from home. It's shameful to wake up late and leave the morning chores,' she replied reflexively, then caught herself. 'But maybe… maybe shame isn't the worst thing to shed.'

Sugandha smiled and sat down beside her.

'I thought Alaska would feel like the end of the world,' Radhika murmured. 'But last night… I thought maybe it's the beginning of something.'

She looked up at the pale orange sky. 'Back home, everything had to have a reason. *Aurat ka kaam toh ghar sambhalna, aur bachche paalna* (A woman's duty is to take care of the house and raise children).' She paused, chuckling dryly. 'But I did all that. And still I was angry. Tired. Alone.'

Sugandha placed a gloved hand over hers. 'We all did. And look at us now. Sitting here like schoolgirls waiting for their final exam results.'

Radhika didn't reply immediately. She was contemplating the old tractor she still kept, despite her son saying it was outdated. She thought of the women in her village who looked at her as if she were a miracle. She remembered the land that still bore her footprints.

'I want to start something,' she said slowly. 'Maybe a school. For village girls. A place where they don't have to be wives first. Maybe I'll give my land to that.'

Sugandha's eyes widened. 'You mean it?'

Radhika smiled. '*Is baar toh sach mein karna hai.* (This time I really want to do it.)'

And in that moment, she wasn't just someone's mother. Or someone's widow. She was simply Radhika—a woman with her own story to write, under her own name.

Radhika continued to walk around long after Sugandha had gone back inside. The snow crunched and melted under her boots, and her breath came out in steady puffs like the rhythm of an old tractor on a winter morning. A school.

This was not a fanciful thought this time. It was not something she muttered to herself in helpless rage or buried in conversations with the dead, asking Virender what to do. It was real now, vivid, like the green of her paddy fields at harvest, like the sparkle in her eyes when she first taught her farmhands to calculate crop yields without a man's help.

She pulled out her phone. Even here, with patchy reception and frozen fingers, she started jotting down ideas. It was not a complete plan—just notes. *Gaon ki chhoriyaan* (village girls), *Kheton se seedh*a school (from farms, straight to schools), practical learning, farming basics, computer education, self-defence, workshops, solar panels, open library…

The thoughts came fast and sure, like they'd been waiting inside her all along.

For so many years, she had fought for land rights, argued with bank officers, and taught herself market trends just to survive. Now, she realised—why not pass that on?

Why sit in a *haveli* waiting for a son to return?

She remembered Kusum, the bright young girl in her village who had dropped out after eighth standard because her mother was unwell, and her brother needed school fees. She remembered standing in her godown, watching boys play with discarded plastic pipes, while their sisters cooked lunch for farmhands.

Her jaw tightened.

'No more of that,' she muttered aloud. '*Bas ho gaya.* (It's enough.)'

The snow around her had stopped falling. In the silence that followed, the world seemed to lean in. Even the wind paused to listen.

She'd start with her own land. Build something small. She had money set aside, meant for her son's return. But maybe it was time to return it to the girls of the land instead.

The school would not be named after Virender. It wouldn't even carry the family surname. No. It would have the name of the first girl to enrol. Let them write their own stories.

A soft rustle behind her—Sonali, wrapped in a shawl and cradling her coffee, called out, 'Still planning to conquer the world before breakfast?'

Radhika laughed a deep, resonant laugh from the gut.

'No. Just trying to ensure some girls never have to wait for anyone to permit them.'

And with that, she stood. Shoulders square. Eyes sharp. The new revolution had begun. Quietly. In snow boots.

Debjyoti

Debu sat on the swing, slightly away from the others, a wool shawl wrapped tightly around her shoulders. The reflection of the Northern Lights rippled in the dark waters like a living dream. She placed one hand over her heart out of reverence.

She had been born with a murmur. Back when surgery meant real risk, when her mother had held her tiny hand in trembling silence, and her father had whispered Tagore's poems like prayers.

Since then, her life has been careful.

No running games. No sharp climbs. No loud rebellions.

She had become the quiet girl, the dependable daughter, the wife who always folded clothes just right, the mother who cooked without complaint, and who ran to America the moment her daughter said, 'Ma, I need help.'

Last night, as they'd sat around the fire, the other women had encouraged her to share her story. She did.

'I always thought if I just stayed calm, stayed grateful, then I wouldn't lose anything else,' Debu had said softly. 'But I did. I lost time. Parts of myself. The artist I was when I was fifteen.'

She hadn't said that out loud in decades. That she used to draw. She had once painted the walls of her room with swirling rivers and trees. Her father had enrolled her in an art class.

And then life had taken over.

But now, with the air tasting like freedom, she made herself a quiet promise.

She would return to Kolkata and paint again. Properly.

She would dig out her old sketchbooks, call the local art teacher who taught seniors in the neighbourhood, buy oil pastels and a proper easel, and sit on her tiny balcony with her tea, sketching the bougainvillaea and the city sky.

And maybe—maybe—she'd even apply to that community mural project her niece had told her about.

Debu smiled at the thought. She was still the woman who cared. But she no longer wanted to be only that. She wanted to create, express, and rediscover the rhythm of her heartbeat.

A light breeze picked up, and she heard footsteps. Radhika sat down beside her. Radhika had just resolved to open a school for the girls in her village and was in a light mood.

'What's going on in that creative mind of yours?' Radhika asked.

Debjyoti chuckled, brushing a strand of grey behind her ear. 'I think I have decided something big. I'm going to paint. Again.'

Radhika's eyes widened. 'That's beautiful.'

'Yes,' Debjyoti said, voice firmer than usual. 'And necessary.'

She looked up. The sky was still dancing.

For the first time in a long, long time, her heart didn't feel fragile. It felt brave.

The cabin had an old wooden swing hanging from a pine beam near the porch. Radhika had wandered indoors, but Debu stayed back. She eased herself into the swing, letting it rock her gently, the creak of the chains syncing with her breath. The night air was sharp, but she didn't mind.

Above her, the sky remained vibrant, green and purple threads swirling like whispers of an ancient dance. She tightened her grip on the shawl and closed her eyes.

She measured time in heartbeats for most of her life, in cautious years and plans put on hold. She lived in low-risk zones—emotional, physical, and even spiritual—the fear of numerous 'what ifs' shaped every decision.

What if her condition flared up again?

What if her daughter inherited it?

What if her husband's mild diabetes turned serious?

What if someone needed her and she wasn't there?

She had carried everyone's health charts in her mind like holy books—cross-referencing symptoms, setting reminders, watching over vitamin doses and checkups. She had never allowed herself the luxury of unplanned days, of selfish wishes.

But tonight, on the swing under the celestial glow, she let the 'what ifs' fall away like autumn leaves.

What if... I lived, really lived?

A breeze tickled her cheek. She opened her eyes and whispered into the night, 'I want to stop worrying so much. About passing on things. About losing things. I've held on so tightly, I forgot how to let things flow.'

She rocked gently.

She would speak to her daughter, not as a caregiver but as a woman. She would tell her, 'You are strong. You are allowed to live without fear.' And she would believe that for herself, too.

She would join that art class. Every Thursday afternoon, even if the doctor's appointments piled up. Even if someone in the neighbourhood said it was a 'waste of time'.

She would allow joy to enter.

The swing creaked once more. She looked out at the trail, the snow glowing faintly.

Maybe she'd even go on a trek someday. Something easy. Somewhere in the hills near Darjeeling. Something for herself.

She touched her chest. She had a scar running right through her midriff. 22 stitches. But like her father's friend Jaspreet, *the Fauji with a scar,* she had come out stronger! She smiled at the thought. I am my father's soldier without a uniform!

This heart had held her back, yes. But it had also kept her going. Now, it was time to let it lead.

She gave the swing one final push with her toes and whispered to the stars,'Thank you.'

Sonali

Sonali stood at the edge of the viewing platform, camera forgotten around her neck, her gloved hands shoved deep into the pockets of her chic white parka. The sky above her was exploding with green ribbons of light. They danced, shimmered, and folded into one another, as if someone had spilt all the world's secrets across the stars.

She had spent her life explaining history—archiving revolutions, lecturing on reformers, and dissecting patriarchy and progress in the same breath—but never had she felt so… rewritten.

In Alaska, she wasn't Professor Sonali Nadkarni. She was just Sonali.

A woman trying to hold her son's truth without fumbling.

Last night, she had whispered the words she hadn't said aloud even to herself.

'I thought Aman's life would look like mine. And now it doesn't. And I'm scared it means he's moving away from me.'

It had come out trembly and small, and Debu had reached across the circle and squeezed her hand, while Mona said, 'That's exactly what makes you a good mom.'

And that was enough. The dam broke. She hadn't cried when she saw Aman's truth that his roommate was actually his partner and they were waiting for the right time to tell her, but here, under the sharp stars and gentle eyes of strangers-turned-sisters, she allowed herself to fall apart. And then, finally, to gather herself again.

Now, Sonali closed her eyes and let the cold kiss her cheeks. She was ready to rewrite the story.

No more measuring motherhood against tradition. No more tallying dreams like attendance sheets. Aman was not an extension of her. He was his own bright, complicated, beautiful soul.

And she—she wanted to be more than just the mother who made peace with that.

She wanted to *celebrate* it.

Her mind, always a flurry of lecture notes and semester plans, now turned to possibility. What if she wrote a new book? *Beyond the Binary: Gender Fluidity and Identity in Ancient Indian Thought.*

What if she started saying *yes* to the things that scared her?

'Sonali?' Sugandha's voice was gentle behind her.

Sonali turned, her profile lit green by the auroras, and smiled. 'It's beautiful, isn't it?'

'Yes. You look like someone who just made a significant decision,' Sugandha said.

'I did,' Sonali replied. 'I'm going to stop apologising for being proud of my son. And of myself.'

She looked up at the sky again, that kaleidoscope of wonder. 'You know, I studied how people change the world all my life. But I think the real magic is letting the world change you.'

Sugandha nodded, slipping her arm through Sonali's as they returned to the warmth. 'Sounds like a good chapter title.'

Sonali grinned. 'I'll save it for the book.'

Back at the cabin, while the others chatted over hot cocoa and peeled off layers of winterwear, Sonali had already pulled out her notebook—the same slim leather-bound one that had followed her to international conferences and coffee shops. But this time, it wasn't filled with citations and course outlines.

This time, she was writing *for herself.*

'Working Title: "Unmothered – Essays on Identity, Modern Parenthood, and Letting Go".'

It had come to fruition—this idea of blending memoir with scholarship—a braided narrative of personal revelations and professional insights. She would speak as both the mother of a queer child and as a scholar of post-colonial India. She would unquestioningly challenge the frameworks she had once taught.

It wouldn't be about Aman. It would be about *her*—a woman raised to hold both bangles and books in balance, now daring to shake the shelves.

She flipped the page and jotted:

- Chapter Ideas:
  - *The Invisible Curriculum of the Indian Daughter*
  - *Queer as Counter-Narrative: A Mother's Unlearning*
  - *Mapping Belonging Beyond Borders: Parenting in Diaspora*
  - *Motherhood Without Possession*

She was already planning leave applications. She'd take a semester off, perhaps spend it in Seattle with Aman and Jake, truly get to know their world, sit in queer bookstores, interview other desi parents, and use her Fulbright contacts to establish dialogues between Indian and diaspora communities. She could feel the hum of something alive inside her—not a return to her younger self, but a reorientation.

Nation, mother, woman—each of them was a construct. Each of them was malleable.

She caught her reflection in the cabin window—windswept and glowing, her eyes bright not with resolve but with curiosity.

She smiled.

'Time to write a new syllabus,' she murmured. This time, her name was at the top—not as a mother or a professor, but simply as Sonali Nadkarni: a *woman, evolving.*

Mona

Mona stood at the edge of a snow-blanketed trail, her breath rising in puffs, eyes still tracing the memory of the sky from the night before. Someone had said that the Northern Lights—

Aurora Borealis—had shimmered like a living thing above them. Like everything she had ever wanted but convinced herself she didn't need.

For once, she had not reached for her phone. No photos. No filters. No forwarding to Neetu with a witty caption. It had felt too sacred to be pinned down by pixels.

Now, walking alone along a frozen ridge near the cabin, she allowed the silence to settle inside her. The only sound was the crunch of her boots in the snow, and the occasional whoop of someone skiing far off. She wasn't dressed for glamour. No statement bag. No lip liner. Just thermal layers and a soul stripped raw from the night's revelations.

Her thoughts circled like snowflakes on the wind. The years of being 'Mom', 'Mona Aunty', 'Mrs Rajput', 'Madam', the woman with the designer shoes, who remembered birthdays and smiled through cracks, no one noticed. The woman who had loved wildly, married young, survived betrayal, and put up with a husband who broke her heart in slow, cruel degrees.

She had believed her job was to remain steadfast for Neetu, to be the fortress. But the truth had settled into her bones in Alaska. Neetu didn't need a fortress; she needed a mother who felt real, who laughed without looking over her shoulder and didn't carry her guilt in designer handbags.

Back at the cabin, Mona made tea alone in the small kitchenette and sat by the frosted window with her cup, watching the pale sun rise over the pines.

She opened her notebook—Neetu's old sketchbook she'd slipped into her suitcase at the last moment. For the first time in years, she began to draw—not large, scared eyes and pouted lips or little houses with a thatched roof like she always did—but loose, joyful sketches—a food truck shaped like a boat. A restaurant with Malaysian and Rajasthani thalis served under a canopy of fairy lights.

Her hands didn't stop. Her heart didn't waver.

When Sonali walked in, Mona looked up with a grin.

'Fairbanks,' she said, tapping her sketchpad. 'That's where I met myself again.'

She caught her reflection in the frosted glass of the window—unkempt hair, faint lines under her eyes, the pigmentation on her face that she always kept covered under layers of concealer, was stark. Instead, she wore a glow that had nothing to do with makeup. This version of her would've made her uncomfortable a few months ago. Unpresentable. But now, she found herself smiling at the woman looking back. She looked… real.

The sketchpad lay open in her lap, the lines bold and unapologetic. The idea was simple. A little café. Not an extension of the posh one she owned now. It would be in some backwaters of Kerala, a mix of her world and her daughter's. Sustainable, warm, welcoming. No faux chandeliers or overdone glamour. Just real food, real people. Like the women who sat beside her last night and saw her without judgment.

For so long, Mona had lived in a state of curated perfection—her social media feeds, her outfits, her parties, and her silence.

But in the hush of the Alaskan night, with the aurora blazing like a celestial uprising, something had changed forever. She remembered the little girl who once wanted to run a food truck and sing Hindi songs off-key with a radio beside her, the teenager who won all the quizzes and debates, who was the star of her school, the young woman who learned to adapt to a zamindar family's expectations—the young wife who turned heartbreak into strength.

She realised now that survival was never supposed to be the end goal. Living—boldly, messily, freely—was.

She got up, poured another cup of tea, and began humming an old Lata Mangeshkar tune under her breath. '*Roz sham aati thi, magar aisi na thi....*' The song reached a high-pitched line that only Lata could sing, '*Yeh aaj meri zindagi mein kaun aa gaya....*' Sonali joined in from the far end of the room. Both went off-key and burst out laughing.

'*Kaun aa gaya nahin, kya ho gaya* (Not "who came, but what happened") in our lives,' Mona corrected her, adapting the lines of the song to their circumstance.

'*Ye aaj meri zindagi mein kya ho gaya....*' They sang and giggled simultaneously.

Sonali walked up to Mona and said, 'You've officially lost your Delhi snoot, Mona.'

Mona laughed—deep and loud, like thunder breaking after a long drought.

'No, darling,' she said, 'I think I've just found my Dehradun mischief again.'

She didn't need Neetu's approval. She didn't need Sandeep's validation. What she needed was already inside her, her rhythm, roots, and fire.

And Mona Rajput, Malaysian-born, Dehradun-schooled, betrayed-but-unbroken, was ready to begin again.

Homeward Bound

The small airport buzzed with tourists headed homeward.

Sugandha shifted her backpack and glanced over her shoulder. 'Girls, I hope no one left anything back at the cabin!'

'Left something?' Mona raised an eyebrow. 'I think we all left a lot behind!'

The others laughed. Radhika was halfway through her chocolate bar, chewing away. Along with Mona, she had developed a taste for chocolates.

'I still can't believe you cried at the swing,' Sonali teased, elbowing Debu.

'I was moved, okay?' Debu replied, mock indignant. 'Also, I hadn't slept.'

'None of us had! Who told us to stay up till 3.00 a.m.?'

'Aurora Borealis,' Mona muttered between bites. 'I like airport snacks—expensive and impulsive.'

They all burst into giggles. Other passengers in the queue turned to look at this bevvy of ladies, some with irritation and some with envy.

A boarding announcement echoed. Seattle. Final call.

'Alright, ladies. Back to real life,' Debu said, pulling on her hoodie.

'No, no, this was real life,' Sugandha replied softly.

They stood for a moment. Quiet. Contemplative.

As they walked toward the gate, Radhika said, 'Next time, let's do Hawaii!'

'Only if no one starts singing "*Roz sham aati thi....*" at 2.00 a.m.,' Debu warned.

'No promises,' Sugandha smiled, tucking the tiny, pressed forget-me-not into her travel diary.

Sonali and Mona nodded vigorously, grinned at each other and started singing, loud and out of key, '*Roz sham aati thi... magar aisi na thi....*'

All the others joined in, '*Ye aaj meri zindagi mein kya ho gaya....*'

Epilogue

The five women you've just met—Sugandha, Sonali, Mona, Debjyoti, and Radhika—aren't just fictional. They're drawn from the women I've known, admired, and learned from. They are parts of me, too. If you know me well, you'll recognise the fragments.

What began as a story about mothers—especially those with children oceans away—became a deeper journey into love, loss, identity, and rediscovery. These women embody what I've seen in countless others: the quiet strength of mothers who guide, worry, protect, and eventually let go.

Sugandha's discomfort with her son's choices mirrors a fear I've often seen—the fear of watching your child outgrow the familiar fabric of home. Sonali feels bittersweet pride watching a child grow into someone unexpected but true to themselves. Debjyoti learns that love isn't duty and that self-care isn't selfish. Radhika demonstrates what it means to start afresh—with grit and grace. Mona experiences the complexity of migration, not just the distance from her child, but also from herself, and then finds her way back.

This isn't just their story. It's a tribute to all women who carry the emotional weight of being everything to everyone, yet often feel they're not enough. But they are.

And so are you.

If there's one thing I've learned writing this, it's that letting go isn't loss—it's freedom. Our roles don't define us; our courage does.

As for the women—

Sugandha began offering cooking classes in Hyderabad, where *pulihora* and *rajma* are equally revered. Radhika's school is halfway completed, and Vikram cannot stop boasting. She has named it after the first girl who enrolled, '*Keerti Navjeevan Shiksha Vidyalaya*'. Sonali is finally writing her book, having secured an advance from a top international publisher. Debjyoti is sitting on her swing in Kolkata, contemplating a name for her grandson, who was born without a hole in his heart. And Mona? She's hiring staff for the restaurant she created on a boat on the backwaters of Kerala. Every plate is rooted in sustainability.

As for me, I'm still trying to let them go.

But maybe, like all women, they're not meant to leave. Just live on—quietly, fiercely—inside us.

The End.

More from The Browser

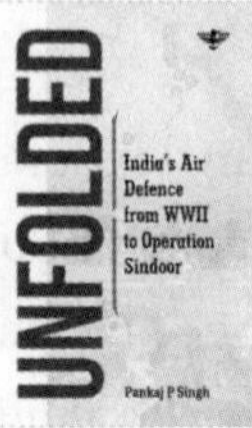

UNFOLDED: India's Air Defence from WWII to Operation Sindoor
Pankaj P Singh
ISBN: 978-93-49042-30-8

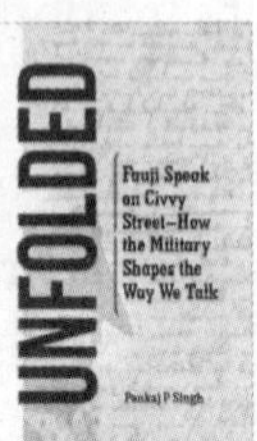

UNFOLDED: Fauji Speak on Civvy Street—How the Military Shapes the Way We Talk
Pankaj P Singh
ISBN: 978-93-49042-98-8

UNFOLDED—How the Audit Trail Heralded Financial Accountability and International Supreme Audit Institutions
P Sesh Kumar
ISBN: 978-93-49042-53-7

UNFOLDED: What Ails India's MSME & Startup Ecosystem?
P Sesh Kumar
ISBN: 978-93-49042-41-4

Inside Fuming Forests
Dr Ira Saxena
ISBN: 978-93-49042-21-6

This Forbidden Thing Called Love
Bubbles Sabharwal
ISBN: 978-93-49042-94-0

Sacred Departures: The Sociology of Death and Dying
Veenat, PhD
ISBN: 978-93-49042-27-8

Kashmir in the Line of Fire: A Memoir of Its Unordinary People and Soldiers
Maj Gen Ranjan Mahajan
ISBN: 978-93-49042-44-5

The Cantonment Ghosts and Other Stories
Ashok Ahlawat
ISBN: 978-93-49042-60-5

Adi Shankara, Advaita and You
Suparna-Saraswati Puri
ISBN: 978-93-49042-05-6

For More Information

More Cuppa Classics

The Trial
Franz Kafka
ISBN: 978-93-49042-88-9

The Story of My Life
Helen Keller
ISBN: 978-93-49042-32-2

The Adventures of Tom Sawyer
Mark Twain
ISBN: 978-93-49042-82-7

Adventures of Huckleberry Finn
Mark Twain
ISBN: 978-93-49042-59-9

Steppenwolf
Herman Hesse
ISBN: 978-93-49042-07-0

A Farewell to Arms
Ernest Hemingway
ISBN: 978-93-49042-76-6

Why I Am an Atheist
Bhagat Singh
ISBN: 978-93-92210-45-7

The Republic
Plato
ISBN: 978-93-49042-15-5

The Idiot
Fyodor Dostoevsky
ISBN: 978-93-49042-49-0

The Great Gatsby
F Scott Fitzgerald
ISBN: 978-93-49042-81-0

The Art of War
Sun Tzu
ISBN: 978-93-92210-79-2

Moby Dick
Herman Melville
ISBN: 978-93-49042-86-5

For More Cuppa Classics